SECRETS AND SHADOWS

Praise for Brian Gallagher's books:

Across The Divide

'The atmosphere of a troubled city awash with tension and poverty is excellently captured'

Irish Examiner

'A compelling historical novel'

Inis Magazine

'Highly recommended'

Bookfest

Taking Sides

'An involving, exciting read ... a first class adventure'

Carousel Magazine

Sunday Independent

plays and short stories have been produced in Ireland, Britain and Canada. He has worked extensively in radio and television, writing many dramas and documentaries. He collaborated with composer Shaun Purcell on the musical, *Larkin*, for which he wrote the book and lyrics, and on *Winds of Change* for RTÉ's Lyric FM.

His first book of historical fiction for young readers was *Across the Divide*, set in the 1913 Dublin Lockout, followed by *Taking Sides,* set against the background of the Civil War, and *Stormclouds*, a tension-filled story of friendship overcoming old differences in 1960s Belfast. Brian lives with his family in Dublin.

SECRETS AND SHADOWS

TWO FRIENDS IN A WORLD AT WAR

BRIAN GALLAGHER

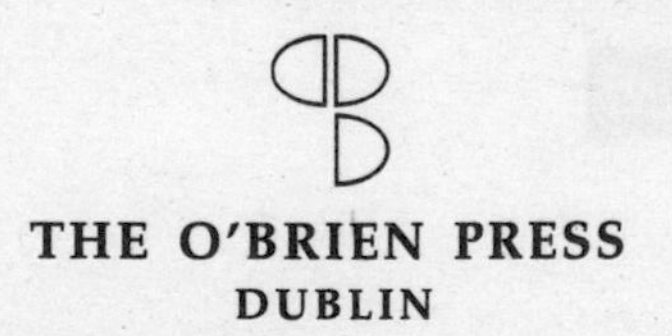

THE O'BRIEN PRESS
DUBLIN

First published 2012 by The O'Brien Press Ltd,
12 Terenure Road East, Rathgar, Dublin 6, Ireland.
Tel: +353 1 4923333; Fax: +353 1 4922777
E-mail: books@obrien.ie
Website: www.obrien.ie
Reprinted 2013.

ISBN: 978-1-84717-350-8

2 3 4 5 6 7 8
13 14 15 16 17

Secrets and Shadows received financial assistance from the Arts Council.

Typesetting, editing, layout and design: The O'Brien Press Ltd
Cover image courtesy of iStockphoto
Printed and bound by CPI Group (UK) Ltd, Croydon, CR0 4YY
The paper in this book is produced using pulp from managed forests

The O'Brien Press receives assistance from

DEDICATION

To the soirée members – Clare, Eugene, Eilish, Declan, Anne and Jerry – a great group of friends.

ACKNOWLEDGEMENTS

My sincere thanks to Michael O'Brien for his enthusiastic support and suggestions when I proposed a children's historical novel set during the Second World War, to my editor, Mary Webb, for her customary insight and advice, to publicist Ruth Heneghan for all her efforts on my behalf, and to the entire staff at The O'Brien Press, with whom it's a pleasure to work.

I'm grateful once more to Annie-Rose O'Mahony and Sean Pardy, two young readers who generously took the time to read the first draft of the book and share their thoughts with me.

My thanks also go to the Arts Council for their bursary support, to Tommy Coyle, Paddy Kelly and Brendan Sheehan at Stanhope Street Convent, to the staff in Pearse Street Library, to Joe Foley for information about Cobh, to Aoife Lucy for research on rationing in 1941, to Cathy Roberts of Fort Perch Rock, New Brighton, for help and advice regarding Liverpool during the blitz, and to Hugh McCusker for his meticulous proof-reading.

And, as ever, the greatest thanks of all go to my family, Miriam, Orla and Peter, for their unflagging support.

PROLOGUE 3 MAY 1941.

17 CEDAR TERRACE LIVERPOOL.

Barry had never felt so frightened. He ran out the hall door, horrified to see that tonight Liverpool was ablaze. The city where he had spent all twelve years of his life had been bombed lots of times, but this was the worst raid yet. High explosive bombs were raining down on the docks, on factories, on the city centre, on housing estates – in fact anywhere the German bombers felt like targeting.

Barry had survived terrible raids coming up to last Christmas, but then in the New Year the attacks had eased off and life had mostly returned to normal. Of course Britain's war with Adolf Hitler and the Nazis went on in other places – his dad was fighting with the Royal Navy somewhere in the Mediterranean – but Liverpool had been spared the frequent heavy raids of last year.

Now, though, the *Luftwaffe* bombers were back with a vengeance, and the air vibrated to the sound of aircraft engines. Barry felt his heart pounding as he followed his mother out the gate of their small front garden while loud explosions filled the air.

The nearest underground air raid shelter was about a quarter of a mile away. Even though his mother could run fairly quickly, that meant they were still going to be exposed while they sprinted through the blacked-out streets.

'Take my hand, Barry!' she cried now as she reached the pavement.

Normally he would have hesitated to hold hands with his mother in public. Her tone didn't allow for argument, though, so he took her hand and ran beside her, the street occasionally lit by the flash of anti-aircraft fire.

In the early days of the war, when bombing and ack-ack fire were still a novelty, Barry and his friends collected pieces of shell casings and the sharp metal bomb fragments called shrapnel. Now shrapnel wasn't a prize to be collected, but something that could cut you in two if you were out on the street when a bomb detonated. Suddenly there was a series of thunderous explosions, nearer this time, though still several streets away. Barry thought of the red hot shrapnel being unleashed and he picked up his speed, his chest heaving as he gulped in smoke-filled air.

'Don't knock me over, Barry!' gasped his mother.

'Sorry, Mum,' he answered, dropping his pace slightly to match her top speed. There was a glow in the sky from where fires were raging all across the city, but the street lamps were off, and every house was in darkness with blackout curtains preventing any light escaping. This was Barry's neighbourhood, however, and despite the blackout he ran unerringly in the direction of the bomb shelter, praying silently that they would make it in one piece.

There were few others on the streets, with most people already having made for the shelters. Barry felt bad, knowing that he had put both Mum and himself at risk by arguing with her about not wanting to go to the smelly, crowded shelter. But this was too big a raid to sit out at home, and now he was sorry he hadn't gone to the underground shelter as soon as Mum had suggested it. He hated having to leave his home, but the Morrison shelter that they had erected in the kitchen wouldn't provide enough protection from heavy bombing like this. His father had joked in one of his letters that the Morrison shelter looked like a big rabbit hutch, and had asked Mum if they would have to eat lettuce when they were using it.

He hadn't seen his father since September, however, when he was last home on leave. He wished that Dad was here. He missed his jokes, and on a night like this he missed the comfort of Dad always seeming to make things right. But there was no point wishing for things you couldn't have. There was just himself and Mum – he had been an only child since his baby sister died – and they had to look after themselves.

They continued running down the road, then turned the corner, heading in the direction of the river Mersey. Despite being anxious to reach the shelter they stopped dead on rounding the corner. The sight before them was breathtaking. A huge anti-aircraft barrage balloon had come adrift from its moorings and was burning furiously, while in the city centre and all along the docks countless fires blazed, with sparks erupting high into the air. Searchlights criss-crossed the sky, trying to locate the bombers, and the sky above Birkenhead, on the far side of the Mersey, was lit up by an angry red glow.

The air carried a smell of burning rubber, and even as they watched, further explosions erupted, reminding Barry of the fireworks displays on Guy Fawkes Night. But these weren't fireworks, these were incendiary bombs and high explosives, and they were killing men, women and children.

'Oh my God,' said his mother, 'there'll be nothing left!'

Barry loved his hometown and tried to console himself with the thought that it had come through other raids. He hoped that the huge statues of the two Liver Birds – the symbols of Liverpool – would survive atop their building at the Pierhead. Right now, though, the priority was to reach safety.

'Let's get to the shelter, Mum,' he said.

'Right,' she answered grimly, then they began to run again.

They went at a fast pace, occasionally encountering others scurrying for safety. Spurred on by the sound of exploding bombs they kept running, their lungs burning. They approached another corner, about a hundred and fifty yards from the shelter. They rounded the corner at speed, almost colliding with a thin elderly woman who stood uncertainly on the edge of the pavement.

'Sorry!' cried his mother as they went to go past.

'Where is it?' called the woman. 'Where is it, love?'

Despite wanting to reach safety, Barry's mother hesitated.

'Where is it, love?' the woman repeated forlornly, her pinched face a picture of confusion.

His mother had stopped now and she turned back to the older woman. 'Where's what, Missus?' she panted.

'The shelter. Where's the shelter?'

'On the left, at the end of this road.'

'I...I got lost,' said the woman. 'Why are...why are they doing this?' she asked, pointing up at the bombers and sounding close to tears.

Barry felt sorry for her. But if they stopped to escort her to the shelter it would take ages. And being exposed for that long could cost their lives. Barry watched his mother put her hand on the woman's arm.

'It's all right, Missus,' she said reassuringly.

Barry remembered the promise he had made to Dad that he would look out for his mother. 'Mum' he said urgently, 'if we delay here–'

'We can't leave her, Barry.'

'But–'

'We can't.' His mother spoke to the woman again. 'Where are your family?'

'I've...I've no family now...'

'Who were you with?'

'Mary. I visited my friend Mary. Why are they doing this?' the woman repeated, again looking up helplessly towards the droning bombers overhead.

'Where's Mary now?' his mother asked, trying to calm the older woman.

'I don't know…I…I don't know…'

'OK. You come with us then.'

'Mum…' began Barry, but his mother raised her hand.

'We have to, pet. It's only right. Take her arm.'

Barry took the woman's bony arm, knowing that there was no point arguing. He had heard his mother saying that Adolf Hitler wanted to destroy the British way of life, and the way to defy him was by not changing, but behaving as decently as ever. And this was what she was doing now, even though she was frightened. They set off again, his mother taking the woman's other arm.

'Are we going to the shelter?' asked the elderly woman.

'Yes. But we *really* need to go as fast as we can.'

Despite being urged on, the woman was maddeningly slow. Barry tried to curb his impatience, knowing it wasn't her fault. Then another stick of bombs exploded deafeningly, just a few streets away. The air was filled with dust, and Barry felt the shock wave from the blast, but he made sure to keep supporting the old woman, and all three of them managed to stay on their feet.

Barry was really scared now, but he tried hard to be brave. His thoughts were in turmoil, part of him admiring his mother for doing the decent thing, but part of him angry at the risk she was taking for a total stranger. How could he face Dad if anything happened to her? It didn't bear thinking about, and he tried to put it from his mind.

They travelled on, passing a vacant lot where houses had been demolished after a previous raid. The garden walls were blown away, and Barry got a glimpse into someone's exposed back garden, illuminated briefly by the light of an exploding anti-aircraft shell. He got an idea, but before he could say anything the old woman turned to his mother.

'Can we rest, please?'

'At the shelter. We can't stay in the open.'

'But I'm tired.'

'I know', said Barry's mother, and he could hear her trying to stay patient. 'But it's too dangerous.'

'I've an idea, Mum!' said Barry. 'You keep going, back in a second.'

Before his mother could object, Barry set off for the vacant lot. Picking his way across the rubble, he headed for the back garden he had seen. There was a faint light from the fire-lit sky, then another burst of anti-aircraft fire illuminated the gloom briefly, and Barry saw what he had come for. A wheelbarrow was propped against the back wall of a standing house, and Barry quickly reached out for it. Normally he wouldn't have dreamt of taking someone's property, but this was a matter of life and death, so he grabbed it. He wheeled it off as quickly as he could across the vacant site and into the roadway. His mother and the old lady had gone only a few more yards, and he swiftly caught up with them.

'Put her in this, Mum!' he said.

The old woman looked at him as though he were mad.

'What?!'

'You just sit on it,' said Barry,' and we'll push you. It'll be much faster.'

'Well done, Barry,' said his mother. Then before the woman could protest they held the wheelbarrow steady and lowered her into it. As if to underline the danger they were in there was another deafening bang. They got a smell of burning oil and felt the blast from the explosion.

'Let's go!' said Barry, and they pushed the wheelbarrow, holding the woman in place and steering with one handle each.

They made much faster progress now, and Barry was pleased that his idea had worked. The shelter was up ahead, and he felt his spirits rising. At the same time he found himself getting more fearful. To have made it this far and then be hit on the last leg of the journey would be unbearable. They kept going, then Barry suddenly cried out in warning. 'Stop, Mum, stop!'

His mother obeyed at once, and they shuddered to a halt. The old woman cried out, but Barry reacted quickly, wrapping his arms around her and holding her gently in place. He got the scent of moth balls from her clothing and felt her bony frame under her coat.

'It's OK,' he said, 'it's OK.'

But it nearly hadn't been. Another couple of feet and they would have gone into a crater where a bomb must have fallen on the road. Barry peered into the dark, anxious to find a route that the wheelbarrow could negotiate. Instead Mum took charge.

'Leave the barrow! It won't get through this. We'll carry her the last bit!'

His mother was right, and without wasting any time he helped the woman from the wheelbarrow, then copied Mum who had draped the woman's right arm around her own shoulder. Barry draped the woman's left arm around his shoulder, then they each put their arms around her tiny waist and lifted her up.

Grunting from the effort, they carried her across the broken ground of the crater. Suddenly an ARP warden came running from the entrance to the shelter. 'Here, I'll take her!' he said. He was a big man, and he swiftly scooped the protesting woman up in a fireman's lift.

'It's all right, Missus,' he told her, 'nearly there!'

Just then another bomb exploded with a loud bang several streets away. 'Right, follow me!' cried the warden and he took off at speed.

Barry and his mother ran after him, and Barry found himself praying under his breath. *Please, God, let us make it after all this!*

They sprinted the last yards towards the doorway of the shelter, then finally their journey was over. The warden ran down the steps, the old woman still on his back. Barry's mother followed behind, but now that they had reached safety, something made Barry pause at the door.

He looked back at the burning city. His relief at arriving unhurt was mixed with fury at what was being done to his hometown. He sensed that life in Liverpool would never be the same after this, and he swore that he would do something to fight back. He had no idea what it might be, but he promised himself that someday he would. Then he breathed out wearily, turned away from the blazing city and descended the steps into the shelter.

PART ONE

ARRIVALS

CHAPTER ONE

4 JUNE 1941, DUBLIN.

Uncle Freddie wasn't funny, but unfortunately he thought he was. He was sitting at the breakfast table and imitating Mr Churchill, the British Prime Minister. Grace wanted to tell him that he didn't sound a bit like the English leader, whom she had often seen on the Movietone News at the cinema. She bit her tongue. Ma had warned her not to complain about anything. Ma said that guests had to adapt to their hosts, not the other way round, and that they must be good house guests while they were staying with Granddad and his son, Uncle Freddie.

Grace loved Granddad, who was soft-spoken and kind. Even Uncle Freddie wasn't too bad when he acted like the electrician that he was, instead of trying to be a comedian. To Grace's relief he ended his impersonation of Mr Churchill, acknowledged their polite laughter, and returned to his breakfast porridge, slurping it slightly in a way that Grace found annoying.

'More tea, anyone?' said Ma.

'Thanks, Nancy, don't mind if I do,' said Granddad.

'Freddie?'

'Sure a bird never flew on one wing, what?' said Freddie, holding out his teacup for Ma to pour.

'You might as well have a hot sup too, love,' said Ma, and Grace nodded in agreement.

Like most twelve-year-olds she wasn't particularly keen on tea, but because of the war it was rationed, so adults hated wasting it once a pot had been made.

They all drank up, and Grace thought how strange it was to be staying here. A week ago she had been living contentedly with Ma in their cottage. She wished that they could return there right this minute. But Ma had always taught her to be positive, so she stopped thinking about how they had been left homeless and tried to feel grateful for the roof over their heads.

'Did I tell you I got three ounces of tobacco last night?' said Uncle Freddie proudly, like this was a big achievement.

'Really?' answered Ma politely.

'Leave it to Freddie, what?!' her uncle continued, happily praising himself.

Great, thought Grace, *now he'll be smoking his smelly pipe even more.*

'How did you manage that?' asked Granddad.

Granddad wasn't a pipe smoker himself, but Grace had noticed that adults were usually intrigued when someone managed to get extra supplies of the things that were scarce because of the war.

'Oh now…' said Freddie, as though he were some kind of man of mystery. Then he couldn't resist boasting and he looked at Grace and winked. 'You scratch my back,' he said.

'Sorry?'

'You scratch my back, and I'll scratch yours.'

'Right...'

Freddie turned to the others now, like a magician revealing a very clever trick.

'Didn't I wire the tobacconist's house last year, and did him a few extra sockets. So I dropped into his shop last night and told him I was gummin' for a smoke.'

'Very subtle, Freddie,' said Granddad with a grin.

'Subtle gets you nowhere. *Ask and you shall receive* – amn't I right, Nancy?'

'I'm sure you are,' said Ma agreeably.

Maybe I could ask him to stop slurping his porridge, thought Grace *– though I know what I'd receive if I did!*

'What's the joke?' said Freddie.

Grace realised that she must have been smiling to herself. Freddie looked at her enquiringly, and she tried not to panic.

'Eh…just…just thinking about a Mutt and Jeff cartoon,' she answered. Mutt and Jeff were cartoon characters in the *Evening Herald* newspaper, and they were the first thing that came into her head.

'Ah yeah, those lads would make a cat laugh, right enough,' said

Freddie, and Grace felt relieved that he accepted her answer.

'Talking about cats,' said Freddie, 'Did I tell you about the aul' wan with the cats in Terenure?'

'You did, yeah,' said Granddad.

'I didn't tell you though, Nancy, did I?'

'No,' answered Ma, and Grace could see that even someone as good natured as Ma had to make an effort to seem eager for one of Freddie's tales this early in the morning. 'What was that, Freddie?' she asked gamely.

Freddie put down his bowl of porridge and leaned forward. 'It's a good one, if I say so myself...'

Freddie began telling a long-winded story, and Grace followed Ma's example, trying for an interested look on her face. Inside she felt differently. *Why do we have to be here?*, she thought, as she wished, with all her heart, that she was back home where she belonged.

* * *

Barry was worried. The class bully, Shay McGrath, had been picking on him during the three weeks that he had been attending his new school in Ireland. Going in the entrance gate a moment ago McGrath had suddenly pushed him for no reason, and Barry feared that today would be a bad day.

It had started off discouragingly when he saw the headline of the newspaper that was delivered to his grandma's house each morning. The paper said that the Greek island of Crete had just fallen to the Nazis, and Barry wondered how the Germans could be stopped as they swept across Europe. What hope was there of his Uncle George being set free from the prisoner of war camp where he was held, unless the Nazis were defeated? And Barry knew that his own father wouldn't get to come home from the Royal Navy unless the Allies won the war and defeated Adolf Hitler.

It was now over eight months since Dad had been home on leave. It seemed like ages ago, and Barry wished they could be together again. He missed the funny songs that Dad sang to make him laugh, and going to football matches together at Anfield, and just having him around the house. But his father's ship was still in action somewhere in the Mediterranean and there was no telling when they would see each other.

Barry missed his mother too, even though it was only three and a half weeks since she had sent him off to Dublin. After the night when they had brought the old woman to the underground shelter Mum had insisted that for safety's sake he go and stay with his grandma in neutral Ireland. That night in Liverpool had been the worst of the war, and the devastation in the city centre the next day was horrific. Lewis's, the famous department store, had taken a direct hit and was gutted, and a ship loaded with a cargo of bombs had exploded in Huskisson Dock, causing such a colossal blast that the two-ton ship's anchor block landed outside Bootle Hospital, a mile and a half away.

During a week of attacks over six hundred bombers had pounded the city, devastated the docks and wrecked the Custom

House, the Liverpool Museum, and many other local landmarks. Thousands of people had been killed and injured, with even more left homeless. But although the raids had been frightening, Barry still hadn't wanted to leave his friends behind.

Mum couldn't be talked out of it, though, and she had bought the ferry ticket and made all the arrangements. Barry had then argued that if Liverpool was that dangerous, she should come to Dublin too. But Mum was stubborn. She worked in a factory manufacturing aeroplane engines for the Royal Air Force, and she explained that she couldn't shirk her part in the fight against Hitler while Dad was risking his life at sea, and Uncle George was locked up in a prison camp.

He remembered her wiping away her tears and trying to keep a smile on her face as she waved him off on the ferry from Liverpool to Dublin. His Grandma Peg, Dad's Irish mother, had gone out of her way to make him feel welcome in Ireland. And he liked Dublin, and had often stayed in his grandma's house in Arbour Hill during the summer holidays. But living here was different. Taken away from his old school and his old friends, he was suddenly the new boy – and an easy target for jeering with his different background and English accent.

He walked into the school yard, the sky overcast, and he nodded to several boys from his class who were gathering for the Tuesday morning drill session with their Polish instructor, Mr Pawlek. Not all the boys in his class were mean to him, and Barry's ability to tell jokes had broken the ice with some of his classmates. But he understood how schoolyards worked, and if a bully like McGrath decided he didn't like someone, then McGrath's gang would go along with it – as would other boys who didn't want to get on the wrong side of a bully.

On Barry's first day in the school McGrath had loudly asked was it not enough to have the English coming over to Ireland for 700 years – without another one of them moving into sixth class. Barry had kept his voice reasonable and answered that thousands of Irish people had been glad to go to England, people like his own dad, who as a young man couldn't find work in Ireland.

McGrath had sneered and said, 'Fine. Let's do a swap. Your aul' fella can come back to Ireland – and you go back to England!'

Some of the other boys had laughed, but Barry had shrugged it off, not wanting to get into a fight with a bigger, intimidating character like McGrath. The annoying thing was that he would have happily gone back to Liverpool in the morning. But he had no choice; his mother had insisted that he had to stay in Dublin.

So here he was, three weeks into his time in Brunner – St Paul's Boys' School in Brunswick Street – with almost four weeks to go before the term ended. He crossed the school yard, the air heavy with the smell from the nearby soap factory. Today was the first school day since the weekend air raid on Dublin's North Strand, and many of the boys were talking about how the Germans had bombed the city, despite Ireland being a neutral country.

'Did you hear the explosions at the weekend?' asked Charlie Dawson, a slight but perky boy who was friendly to Barry when

McGrath wasn't around.

'Yes,' answered Barry, 'they woke us up.'

'I heard the army were firing up green, white and orange flares – so the pilot would know he was over Ireland.'

'Really?'

'That's what they're saying,' said Charlie. 'Didn't work though, did it?'

'No, I suppose not.'

'My da went down there the next day. Said the damage was desperate – he never saw anything like it.'

He should have seen Liverpool, thought Barry, though he was careful not to say it. Although the attack by one aeroplane on Dublin was tiny compared to the massive raids on his hometown, it was still terrible for the people who had been killed and injured at the North Strand.

'All right, boys, form a line!' said McGrath as he approached. He said it in imitation of the foreign accent of Mr Pawlek, and the other boys laughed at McGrath's mimicry.

Even though he didn't want to antagonise the class bully, Barry couldn't bring himself to join in. For one thing Mr Pawlek was fair-minded and popular – and he had been particularly welcoming to Barry as a new boy. There was also the fact that Barry too had a different accent to the rest of the boys, so he wouldn't make fun of the drill teacher's grammatically correct but accented English.

McGrath approached Barry, aware that he wasn't laughing. 'No sense of humour, Malone?'

Barry wasn't going to apologise for not going along with the joke, but neither did he want to provoke the bigger boy, so he said nothing.

'Anyone ever tell you that?' persisted McGrath.

Still Barry refused to be drawn, and now McGrath sneered and mimicked his Liverpool accent.

'Anyone ever tell you there's something wrong with the talking part of your brain?' he said.

'Anyone ever tell you you're a pain?' snapped Barry, unable to take any more goading.

Several of the other boys looked surprised, and Charlie Dawson said 'That even rhymes!'

'Yeah we get it, Dawson,' said McGrath, aggressively turning on him.

'I'm…I'm only saying,' answered Charlie.

'Well, don't say. And you, Malone,' said McGrath, turning to Barry. 'Think you're smart, don't you?'

Barry racked his brains for an answer that wouldn't sound like giving in, but that also wouldn't make things worse.

'Everything all right, boys?' said a voice, then Mr Pawlek casually stepped between them. He was muscularly built, with sandy brown hair and clear blue eyes, and he moved with the ease of a natural athlete.

'Everything is fine, sir,' said Barry with relief.

Mr Pawlek looked enquiringly at McGrath, who held his gaze briefly, then nodded.

'Yeah, fine, sir,' he said.

'Right, put aside your bags and form a line,' said the drill teacher.

Barry turned away from McGrath without another word and placed his schoolbag against the wall. This time he had been saved by Mr Pawlek, and with luck the incident might blow over. But he sensed that his smart answer had made McGrath more of an enemy than ever, and he feared there would be trouble ahead.

Was Uncle Freddie going to slurp his way through every meal? Grace wondered as she sat at the kitchen table. Admittedly, Ma's stew tasted delicious, but Granddad and Ma were able to enjoy it without making the irritating noises that Freddie made.

The evening sunshine shone in through the kitchen window, and Grace let its warmth play on her face as Granddad talked about the dance orchestras that he listened to on the wireless. She had noticed that Granddad and Uncle Freddie seemed to argue about everything, but without ever actually getting annoyed, and now Granddad was making a case for the Joe Loss Orchestra while Freddie claimed that Joe Loss wasn't in the same league as Mantovani and his orchestra.

Grace couldn't be bothered following the argument and she let her mind drift, then with a jolt she realised that her mother was talking to her.

'Grace? You're away with the fairies.'

'Sorry, Ma.'

'I said, did you want more stew?'

'No thanks, Ma, I'm grand.'

She wasn't, really. Or at least she would have been a lot *more* grand if she were wearing her own clothes instead of her cousin Geraldine's cast-off dresses and shoes. But the bombing of the North Strand had wrecked their cottage, and every scrap of clothes that she owned and all their furniture had been destroyed. It was what her mind had just drifted back to – something that was happening a lot since her life had been turned upside down by the air raid.

It was four days now since the bombing, and Grace and Ma had spent the first night in a crowded school hall with dozens of other people whose homes had been demolished. The seriously injured had been taken to hospital, and everyone else had been provided with food and blankets, while first aid was given to the many people like Grace and Ma who had suffered minor cuts and bruises.

The next day Grace's Aunt Cissy had arrived with spare clothes for them both, and Grace had been relieved to leave the noisy, crowded hall. Cissy lived with her husband and five children in a small cottage in Coolock, so there wasn't really room there for two more people. And so Grace and Ma had come to Granddad's house.

Ma had said that there were two ways of looking at this. You could say they had been really unlucky to lose their home and everything in it. Or you could say they had been blessed to walk out of it in one piece. Ma always looked on the bright side, so she felt that they were blessed, and when Grace thought of all the people who had been killed and injured, she had to agree.

It was good, too, the way Ma always tried to find the fun in any situation. She said that because Granddad's house was near the cattle market Grace would be able to enjoy the drovers herding cattle along Stoneybatter – where the animals sometimes ran amok – and because they were also near the Phoenix Park they could go to watch the polo there, or to see the dogs swimming in the dog pond.

Ma wasn't just a dreamer, though, she also got things done. Already she had enrolled Grace in the nearby Stanhope Street convent. It was too far to get to Grace's old school at North Strand, but although there was less than a month to go until term ended, Ma had insisted that Grace couldn't miss school. And Ma and Granddad had combined to get Grace a part-time job, with Granddad persuading a friend who ran a local cake shop to hire Grace, starting tomorrow.

'Well, that hit the spot,' said Granddad now, ending his argument with Uncle Freddie about the orchestras, and pushing away his plate.

'Yeah, fair play to you, Nancy,' said Freddie, looking approvingly at Ma. 'Us aul' bachelors aren't used to having a good cook like yourself around the place.'

Ma smiled at the compliment, and Grace felt uneasy. Ma had

always said Freddie was a confirmed bachelor. He had a good job as an electrician with the Electricity Supply Board, but he had never married, never even left home, and now in his late forties he was set in his ways. So why was he flattering Ma, the way Grace had seen fellas do when they wanted to impress girls? Surely he couldn't be thinking about Ma that way? It wasn't that Ma wasn't goodlooking – she had flashing brown eyes, and dark hair and sallow skin like Grace's. And though she was fifty now her face looked young and she had no grey in her hair. And widows did sometimes marry again. But still. *Uncle Freddie.* No, she was probably imagining it.

'I see the Army Band is playing in the Hollow next weekend,' said Granddad.

'Really?' said Ma.

The Hollow was a little valley with a bandstand, just inside the Phoenix Park. As a lover of brass bands, Granddad went there regularly.

'Sure maybe we'd all wander up to see them,' suggested Uncle Freddie, raising an eyebrow and looking at Ma.

Grace looked at her mother, hoping she would politely decline.

Ma hesitated, then she nodded casually. 'Yeah, maybe we will.'

No! thought Grace, although she was careful to keep her feelings from showing. Even though she was grateful to Granddad for taking them in and making them welcome, she hated the idea of being away from her friends over the summer. And now, to make things worse, Uncle Freddie sounded like he might be taking a shine to her mother. It didn't bear thinking about. And maybe she was reading it wrong. But she wasn't looking forward to the next few weeks.

'I couldn't, Grandma!' said Barry, putting aside his teacup and looking appealingly at his grandmother.

'Of course you could, love,' she answered, clearing away the crockery after their evening meal.

'I can't just go and knock on their door. I've never met them.'

'Sure aren't the Ryans one of my oldest neighbours? I was talking to Thomas. I said I'd send you down.'

'But, Grandma...'

'No making strange, Barry. They're expecting you. The Ryans are lovely people; you'll be welcome as the flowers in May.'

Barry hesitated. It wasn't that he was shy – he had always been good at telling jokes – but he felt really uncomfortable calling on his own to people he had never met.

'Maybe we could both go?' he suggested.

'No,' said Grandma, 'then it would be like we were visiting. I don't want them having to use their rations feeding us. Better you just pop down.'

Barry tried to think of an objection, but before he could, his grandmother continued.

'Go on. Yourself and young Grace will be company for each

other. You've both had to move home because of the war. You'll have plenty to talk about.'

Barry didn't like to say that the last thing he wanted was to talk about being bombed. He still had nightmares about the roaring fires that raged across Liverpool when the city had been blitzed. He still remembered the distraught look on the face of Georgie Wilson, a boy in his class whose older sister had been killed when a bomb shelter had taken a direct hit, with forty-two lives lost. And it was enough worrying about Mum still being in Liverpool without this Grace girl reminding him of the havoc the German bombers could unleash. He said none of this to Grandma, knowing that she fretted about him, and not wanting to add to her concern.

Grandma smiled her kindly smile and put her hand on his shoulder. 'I bet you'll get on great – you'll have loads in common,' she said.

Barry thought this was crazy. It was like claiming that if he met another boy with fair hair and freckles they would automatically be friends. But there was no point saying this to Grandma. She had already set this up, and he would have to go through with it.

'All right,' he answered. 'When did you fix it for?'

'I didn't say. But now would be a good time.'

Barry hesitated again, and Grandma smiled encouragingly. He nodded, knowing he was beaten.

'OK,' he said, 'I'll call down.'

'Bit of a sweet tooth, have you, Grace?' said Uncle Freddie, resting his elbows on the kitchen table as he looked at her enquiringly.

'Eh, yeah, I suppose so,' Grace answered, unsure where this was leading. They had just finished their meal, but she hadn't eaten any more of Ma's tasty scones than any of the adults, so what was Freddie going on about?

'Most kids love sweet things,' said Freddie, 'but I don't. So maybe we could do a deal.'

'What kind of deal?'

'When they bring in this sugar rationing they're talking about, I could give you some of my sugar.' He looked at Grace and Ma. 'For some of your tea ration – I like a decent brew in work.'

'You're not taking anyone's tea ration!' said Granddad.

'No one said anything about *taking*. I'm talking about *swapping*.'

'You swap marbles when you're ten, Freddie. You're forty-eight – catch yourself on.'

Grace wanted to laugh but she kept a straight face. Sometimes it was enjoyable when Granddad and Freddie sparred, and Grace was looking forward to Freddie's retort when Ma spoke.

'Grace and I would be happy to share. And there's no need for any swapping, you've been more than kind to us.'

'Well done, Freddie,' said Granddad sarcastically, 'put our guests under a compliment, why don't you?'

'That's not what I meant at all,' protested Freddie. 'I just think...'

But whatever Freddie thought never got said, because there were three knocks on the front door, stopping Freddie in mid-sentence.

'Would you ever get that, love?' said Granddad.

'All right,' said Grace, rising from her chair and going out into the hall. She passed the small mahogany table on which Granddad always left his keys and his cap, then reached the hall door and opened it.

A boy of about her own age stood on the doorstep. He had fair hair and a freckled face and greeny-blue eyes that looked at her slightly sheepishly.

'Are you Grace?' he said, in an English accent.

'Yes,' she answered, wondering how he could have known her name. 'Who are you?'

'I'm Barry.'

He said it as though that explained everything. When Grace was slow in responding he elaborated a little awkwardly. 'My eh… my grandma sent me. Your granddad invited me.'

'Oh. Right. Well, come in, so,' said Grace.

He nodded and stepped into the hall. Grace led the way back into the kitchen.

'Granddad, this is Barry.'

'Ah, Barry, you're welcome, son,' said her grandfather, rising and shaking the boy's hand. 'This is the lad I was telling you about, Freddie, Mrs Malone's grandson, from Liverpool.'

'Oh right,' said Freddie. 'Now I have you.' He turned back to the boy and nodded. 'Good man yourself.'

'And this is Grace's mother,' said Granddad, 'Mrs Ryan.'

'How do you do, Mrs Ryan,' said the boy, politely shaking hands.

'I forgot to mention to you, Nancy, that Mrs Malone has Barry here staying for a bit,' said Granddad. 'She thought himself and Grace might be company for each other.'

'Great,' said Ma, 'that would be nice.'

Grace felt annoyed that this had been set up and nobody had told her. And now they were talking about her like she wasn't here. She wanted to say something that wouldn't be quite rude, but that would let them know that she could make her own friends. Before she got a chance, Granddad pointed to the front room.

'Why don't you bring Barry into the parlour and play the gramophone for him?' he suggested.

'OK.'

Her grandfather had a big Pye gramophone of which he was proud, and Grace thought that playing a few records wasn't such a bad idea, and would be easier than being sent out to play with a boy she didn't know.

'Would you like a scone first, Barry?' said Ma.

'No thanks, we've just had tea,' he answered.

'Right, in you go, so,' said Granddad nodding towards the parlour.

Grace led the way, and the boy followed her wordlessly into the front room. He closed the door, then looked at Grace.

'They never told you I was coming?'

'No.'

'I thought it was all arranged.'The way he said it, it sounded like a complaint, but Grace felt that she was the one with the right to complain.

'It *was* arranged,' she retorted. 'They just didn't bother telling me.'

'Right. Well, seeing as we're here, what records have you got?'

His accent was different to the posh English accents that Grace heard on the radio when Ma listened to the BBC, and his voice seemed to go down at the end of sentences, in a way that Grace found a little strange.

'I don't have any records,' she answered, 'these all belong to Granddad and Uncle Freddie.'

Barry had already begun to sift through the records, reading the artists' names from the printed sleeves.

'God, I believe you,' he said.

'What's that supposed to mean?'

'It's old people's music, isn't it? "The Bluebell Polka"? "The Gondoliers"? 'Brass Band Favourites"?"

Even though these *were* old fashioned, Grace felt obliged to defend Granddad. 'There's good stuff too. "Over the Rainbow" is a great song,' she said, indicating the record sleeve with its picture of Judy Garland.

'Yeah, that one's good,' said Barry.

'And "Red Sails in the Sunset" is good too.'

'It's not bad. But in Liverpool we get lots of ships from America

– so we know all the latest stuff.'

'Really?' said Grace, slightly irked by the way he made himself sound superior. 'What's so great about the latest stuff from America?'

'It's just brilliant. I heard the record of Glen Miller doing "In the Mood" before it was even played on the radio.'

'Yeah?'

'And Louis Armstrong with "When the Saints go Marching in".' And Gene Autry. Have you heard him singing "Blueberry Hill"?"

'No – but I've walked up Christchurch Hill.'

It was a smart answer, but Grace had become a bit fed up with Barry's boasting. To her surprise he smiled briefly at her retort.

'OK,' he replied. 'I'm just saying that great tunes come from America, and we get lots of them first in Liverpool.'

He had a nice smile, Grace thought, even if he was a bit cocky. But still, that didn't mean she wanted him as her friend. Adults were in charge of most things in life, but the one thing they couldn't do was decide who your friends were.

He returned to going through the records, then raised an eyebrow as though surprised at what he found. "You are my Sunshine" by Jimmie Davis. That's a decent one.'

'Glad you approve,' said Grace.

If Barry picked up on the sarcasm he chose not to acknowledge it. Instead he handed her the record.

'Want to try it?' he said.

Grace took it from him but didn't put it on. He wasn't going to come in here and be the boss. 'We'll play it after this,' she said, taking up another record.

'What's that?' he asked.

' "When You Wish Upon a Star". I really like it,' said Grace, and she looked him in the eye, as though daring him to run it down. He held her gaze, and she sensed that there was going to be an argument. Then he nodded and suddenly smiled again.

'Good choice,' he said.

Grace was taken by surprise, so she made no response and instead put on the record. She wasn't sure what to make of this Barry Malone. He was unpredictable, one moment annoying, the next moment likeable. Well, she wasn't going to worry about it, she decided. So she sat on the sofa, listened happily to the lilting melody, and wondered how long she would have to stay here keeping him company.

CHAPTER TWO

'Right turn, arms lift, full stretch – and down!'

Barry did the final exercise in the outdoor drill session, then lowered his arms and relaxed, the air in the schoolyard sweet this morning with the smell from a local bakery.

'Very good, boys, dismissed!' cried Mr Pawlek.

Barry watched as the drill master moved among the pupils, exchanging a greeting here and a word of encouragement there. He had the knack of being friendly to the boys yet at the same time wielding the kind of authority that meant nobody messed about during his drill classes.

He came towards Barry now and nodded in greeting. 'So, Mr Malone,' he said with a hint of playfulness in his use of the word mister, 'how are you finding life in Dublin?'

'Fine sir,' answered Barry, impressed again at how fluent Mr Pawlek's English was. Barry had heard Polish spoken back in Liverpool, and it sounded to him like a language that was very different to English, so Mr Pawlek must have studied hard.

'I'm glad to hear it,' continued the teacher. 'It can be a little strange coming to a new country.'

'Yes, sir, though Ireland isn't really new to me. I've often visited my grandmother before.'

'Good. Every boy should be spoiled by his grandmother,' the

teacher said smilingly.

Barry smiled in return, then saw Shay McGrath over the teacher's shoulder. He had kept well away from the other boy since McGrath had attempted to bully him yesterday, but now McGrath caught his eye. McGrath put out his tongue at Barry and made licking gestures. He was being mocked, with McGrath suggesting that he was licking up to the teacher. But what was he supposed to do if Mr Pawlek was being friendly? Not smile, in case a bully like McGrath thought he was trying to win favour? He decided to ignore the other boy's insult and returned his gaze to the drill master.

'It must be hard, away from your parents,' said Mr Pawlek sympathetically. 'Do you often hear from your father?'

'Not too often, sir,' said Barry.

'Where is he serving?'

'Somewhere in the Mediterranean. He can't tell us where.'

'Ah, right. Still, I'm sure his ship will return to England soon.'

'I hope so, sir,'

'And your mother isn't too far away. She'll probably visit regularly.'

'It's not that easy, sir. She can only really come when she takes holidays from work.'

'Of course. So many women working now, with the men off at war. What is she doing?'

'She's a riveter in a factory.'

'Really? What does she make?'

Mr Pawlek said it casually, his light blue eyes looking at Barry in enquiry.

Barry hesitated briefly. Mum's job was in an aircraft factory, and people were always being told not to gossip about anything to do with the war effort. 'Loose lips sink ships' was the phrase on the government warning posters that urged people not to discuss military matters. But Grace Ryan had asked Barry all about Mum's job when they had listened to records yesterday, and Mr Pawlek was looking at him now with the same kind of sympathetic curiosity. 'She's making aeroplane parts for the RAF,' Barry answered.

'Spitfires, is it?'

Barry was surprised at the extent of Mr Pawlek's interest. But then again he was Polish, and Poland had been invaded by the Nazis, so it was understandable that he would be interested in how Britain's Royal Air Force was waging war on Germany.

'No, sir, Hurricanes mostly.'

'A fine aircraft, the Hurricane. And brave of your mother to stay in Liverpool after the bombing. Is she working in the city itself?'

'No, she works outside town. She has to get a bus.'

'I was in Liverpool years ago,' said Mr Pawlek. 'Great city. What part does she get the bus to?'

'I'm not sure, sir. I just know it takes about twenty minutes.'

Mr Pawlek looked as though he was going to ask another question, but then he hesitated and nodded instead. 'Very good. Well, I hope your mother gets holidays soon.'

'Me too, sir.'

'And a word of advice?'

'Sir?'

'I believe you're quite good at football. Follow that up. Sport is a good way for someone ... someone from outside to gain acceptance. Do you understand?'

'Yes, Mr Pawlek. And thanks ... thanks for the advice.'

'You're welcome.' The drill master nodded in farewell, then moved off across the school yard.

Barry stood unmoving for a moment, lost in thought. The conversation had gone in directions that he hadn't expected. And as for the advice about gaining acceptance – did the teacher know that McGrath had been picking on him? Before he could consider it any more the bigger boy approached.

'How's it goin' – fishface?!'

Barry didn't answer.

'Cat got your tongue, Malone? You'd plenty to say a minute ago when you were being teacher's pet.'

Barry was tempted to argue but sensed that it would be better to ignore the other boy's comments.

'Maybe licking up to teachers is what you do in England,' said McGrath. 'But we don't do it here. So catch yourself on. Or better still, go back to where you came from.' He turned away and pushed past Barry, deliberately shouldering him.

Barry regained his balance and watched him go, knowing that sooner or later he would have to deal with the other boy's bullying. The problem was, he didn't know how he could.

CHAPTER THREE

'Try every cake in the shop!' said Nellie.

Grace looked at her new boss disbelievingly.

'Not all at once, of course. But you need to know everything we make. It's easier to sell to customers when you can recommend things yourself.'

'Great,' said Grace, 'I'll work my way through them all.'

It was Grace's first day in the bakery. She was being trained in by the owner, Nellie Kinsella, a tall, thin woman in her sixties who was a friend of Granddad's. For someone so tall, Nellie moved with quick, jerky motions, and she had a habit of staring people directly in the eye when giving her views. She had never married, and Granddad had said that her two passions in life were playing cards and smoking Sweet Afton cigarettes. Grace thought that she was going to like her. And despite the older woman's quirky manner, Grace was impressed – after all, there weren't that many women who ran their own businesses.

Nellie had shown her around the back of the shop, where flour was stocked in large brown sacks and where she baked the bread and cakes in a big oven. Grace had been intrigued to know how her boss managed to get supplies of scarce ingredients, and Nellie had explained that in running a business she was entitled to an industrial quota of rations – although sometimes supplies were interrupted and she had to bake items that required less fruit, or sugar, or whatever other ingredient ran short because of the war.

Now she had finished showing Grace the way to work the cash register and how to keep track of the stock. Grace looked at the tempting rows of rhubarb and apple tarts, jam slices, gur cakes and scones. She was looking forward to trying some of them, but for now she gave her attention to Nellie, who was about to leave her alone in the shop for the first time.

'So remember, Grace, the customer is always right – even though half the time they're eejits and they're wrong. But when they come in here they're right, and we're nice to them.'

'OK.'

'On the other hand, you have to have your wits about you. Most people are honest, but there's some would take the eye out of your head. Do you follow?'

'Yes. The customers are always right – but watch them like a hawk.'

Nellie smiled. 'Now you have it. I'll be back to lock up.'

'All right, Miss Kinsella.'

The older woman crossed the shop in several jerky strides, then exited into the busy thoroughfare of Manor Street, leaving Grace alone behind the counter.

Grace looked at the rows of cakes and felt her mouth watering. The last five days had been tough, what with losing her home in the air raid and then having to start from scratch in a new school. But as part-time jobs went this was a pretty good one, so maybe her luck was turning. And right now the only decision was whether to have a jam slice or a slab of gur cake. Maybe she would have both. But which to try first? She thought a moment, then went to the cash register and pressed the key, as Nellie had taught her. The machine rang, and the till opened. Grace reached in and took out a penny, then quickly tossed it. *Heads for gur cake, harps for a jam slice.* It was heads. She replaced the penny and shut the till, took up a slice of juicy-looking gur cake and raised it to her mouth. No, she thought, this wasn't a *pretty good* job – this was a *brilliant* job!

Barry walked contentedly along the street. Today had been a good day. In school there had been no trouble with Shay McGrath, and he had scored a really stylish goal for his team in a schoolyard football game. The morning had begun well with a letter from his mother. It contained a ten shilling note and lots of news from Liverpool. The most exciting thing for Barry however was the details that his mother sent regarding the Royal Navy's sinking of the biggest, fastest ship in the German navy, the battleship *Bismarck*. The Germans had boasted that *Bismarck* was unsinkable, but Mum had explained how a fleet of British vessels and aircraft had pursued it for over seventeen hundred miles, finally sinking it west of Land's End.

Barry thought of his father, and hoped that his ship had been involved in the victory. It would help to make up for all the months in which he had missed Dad if his vessel had been involved in this blow against the Nazis.

Lost in his thoughts, Barry continued along the busy thoroughfare of Stoneybatter, the late afternoon sunshine bathing the fronts of the shops and pubs along the street in golden light. He walked on past where Stoneybatter became Manor Street, then stopped at the shop known as Miss K's. He checked that he had the half crown his granny had given him, then stepped into the bakery. To his surprise he saw Grace Ryan behind the counter.

'Oh...it's you!'

'Who did you expect?' she answered.

'Miss Kinsella. Doesn't matter – it's the cakes I came for.'

'Right.'

'Sorry. That sounded a bit...what I mean is...'

'It doesn't matter who serves you, once you get your cakes?'

Was she annoyed with him? Barry hadn't meant his comment about the cakes to sound blunt, but surely it wasn't that bad? He thought back to a couple of days ago when he had listened to records with Grace. He had had mixed feelings then about her. She seemed like she was good fun in some ways, but she had been a bit narky too. Though maybe that was because – like himself – she didn't like grown-ups trying to decide who her friends should be. Or was she just a difficult person? He looked at her now, not sure what to think.

Suddenly she smiled. 'Don't worry,' she said, 'you'll get your cakes.'

Barry found himself smiling back, relieved that his awkward-sounding comment hadn't caused a problem after all.

'I can recommend the gur cake,' she said. 'It's gorgeous.'

Barry looked at the thick slabs of gur cake with their juicy dark brown filling, and he was tempted, but he shook his head. 'My grandma sent me to get an apple tart. I better not buy anything else.'

'Fair enough,' said Grace, taking his money and giving him back a wrapped apple tart and his change. 'Do you like jam slices?' she asked.

'Yeah, but like I said…'

'Your grandma told you to buy a tart – I know.'

Grace took up a sharp-looking carving knife, and Barry wondered what she was up to.

'I get to sample all the cakes,' she continued. 'So, fancy sampling half a jam slice?'

'Well…'

'Of course you do!' laughed Grace, then she swiftly cut a jam slice in two and handed him one portion.

'Thanks.'

'You're grand. Sure all you're doing is helping me learn our range of cakes, right?' She winked, then popped half her piece into her mouth.

'Right,' said Barry, with a grin. Then he happily followed Grace's example, bit into the jam slice, and thought that maybe they could be friends after all.

CHAPTER FOUR

Grace tossed and turned in feverish sleep, reliving the events of last week in a vivid dream. Once more she heard the bomber flying over the North Strand and her heart pounded. She pressed her face anxiously up to the window pane and scanned the night sky. She couldn't see anything, but the droning of the plane became louder, and she felt her pulses racing.

Grace wanted the comfort of her mother, but she was too proud to call out. Ma had gone into the kitchen, and Grace thought that she was too old now to be calling for her mammy. It would have been good to still share the bedroom with her older sisters, but there was just herself and Ma living in the cottage now, what with Da dead and her older brothers and sisters all left home.

Suddenly there was a deafening explosion. The next thing Grace knew she was coming to in the gutter outside her house, not knowing for a few seconds where she was. She tried moving her arms and legs. They felt sore, but apart from some grazes and scratches she seemed uninjured.

She looked around in horror and saw that many of her neighbours' houses had been wrecked. There were clouds of dust in the air and she saw bloodied bodies lying further down the roadway. A dead dog lay in the middle of the street and the tattered remains of someone's wedding dress had been blown into the far gutter.

She could hear young children screaming in terror and injured adults moaning and crying out in pain. The realisation of injured people suddenly clarified her muddled thoughts and her stomach tightened in fear. *Ma! Where was Ma?*

Grace rose and ran towards the house. The doorway was completely collapsed, so she climbed over the rubble of the threshold and was able to pick her way across what used to be their living-room. There was dust everywhere, making it hard to see, but part of the wall of the kitchen was still standing, and she made her way as quickly as she could towards it.

She went through what was left of the doorway, then stopped in her tracks. A body lay on the floor. Grace recognised the fawn cardigan that Ma had slipped on over her nightdress. She wanted to scream, but in the way that often happened in nightmares she couldn't make a sound. *Oh, no, please, God,* she thought, running to where her mother lay and falling to her knees beside her. She remembered how awful it had been when Da had died suddenly, and the idea of losing Ma as well was too much to bear. She felt her tears beginning to well up, then suddenly her mother blinked.

'Ma!' she cried.

Her mother opened confused eyes. 'Grace...'

'Oh thank God!' said Grace, throwing her arms around her.

They stayed there for a moment, hugging each other tightly, then they rose and Grace held her mother's hand as they made their way out onto the street. The roadway was full of injured people, and there was screaming and sobbing from adults and children alike. Ma looked aghast at the desolation. The street was covered from end to end with rubble from collapsed houses. Along the centre of the North Strand, the area's main thoroughfare, Grace could see the tram tracks mangled out of shape and pointing grotesquely into the sky.

Suddenly she heard the sound of bells and guessed that it must be fire brigade or civil defence vehicles approaching at speed. She saw Ma staring at the remains of their house and shaking her head disbelievingly. Grace suspected that they were both thinking the same horrible thought – that they might never again live in their happy home.

Grace was about to turn away when something protruding from the collapsed brickwork of the cottage caught her eye. She looked again and saw that it was Fido, the toy wooden dog that her da had carved for her when she was small. It was the only link back to her father, and she wasn't going to let the people who had destroyed her home take that from her too. Before Ma could object, she ran back to the remains of the house, clambering over the broken bricks to get to the toy dog.

'Grace! What are you doing?' cried Ma.

'It's Fido. I'm not losing him too!' she called back, before extracting the toy, which was battered but still in one piece

'The rest of the roof could fall down!' cried Ma. 'Come out this minute!'

Just then there was a rumble, and Grace looked up in horror as the roof collapsed, burying her in rubble. Grace felt suffocated and screamed in terror, then awoke with a start. She realised that she had only been dreaming, and she looked over at Ma in the other bed, still asleep. At least she hadn't screamed out loud and woken everyone. She sat up in bed, her heart pounding, and wiped the perspiration from her forehead. She stayed there, unmoving, as her heartbeat gradually returned to normal, then eventually she lay down again and tried to sleep, praying that she wouldn't have the dream again.

Someone had told her that you never have the same dream twice in the one night. She hoped that this was true, as she lay with closed eyes, trying not to think any more about the most terrifying night of her life.

CHAPTER FIVE

Barry sang along with the closing hymn, but today it was a struggle. Each Sunday morning he went to Mass with his grandmother, and normally he liked the atmosphere in the garrison church, with its stained glass windows and aroma of incense. It was an army chapel attached to Collins Barracks, but civilians were allowed to attend services, and his grandma and many of her neighbours got Mass there each week.

Barry thought it was more interesting than a normal church, especially when he could glance up at the choir loft, where inmates from Arbour Hill Military Prison were brought under escort to attend Mass. This morning, though, Barry's mind was elsewhere. After Communion the priest had suggested that people pray for their special intentions. Barry prayed as usual for Dad away at sea, for Mum's safety in Liverpool and for Uncle George in the prison camp in Germany. And without warning he felt a piercing stab of homesickness for his scattered family. Even though Grandma was really nice to him, he suddenly felt really sad that they were all separated.

There was a lump in his throat, and he had to blink back the tears from his eyes. The welling up of emotion had taken him by surprise, especially since he had been away from home almost four weeks and so far he hadn't given in to homesickness. Steeling himself, he tried hard now to sing along normally with the final hymn, not wanting anyone to see his upset.

He lowered his head a little as though in reverence, and discreetly wiped his eyes. He glanced around the church, anxious that Grace shouldn't see him looking teary-eyed.

He had met her a couple of times since the day she had shared the jam slice, and the more he got to know her the more he liked her. Somehow she seemed to combine a no-nonsense manner with a real sense of fun. He had also started to be accepted in the schoolyard as a good footballer, so it wasn't as though he wasn't settling in to life in Dublin. But for whatever reason he had suddenly missed his mum and dad. It was the kind of thing that Grace might actually understand, but still, he didn't want a girl to see him looking upset.

Barry looked across the aisle to where he had earlier spotted Grace's granddad and her uncle Freddie. He didn't see Grace and her mother, however, and as the congregation finished the hymn people genuflected and began to make for the exit doors of the church.

Barry and Grandma followed the crowd, and Barry hoped that they could avoid the Ryans today. Grace's granddad was nice enough, but her uncle Freddie was what Irish people called an eejit, and Barry definitely wasn't in the humour for him this morning. Barry reached the door and stepped out into the fresh morning air. He was descending the steps with his grandmother when he heard his name being called.

'Mr Malone.'

There was only one person who ever called him that, and Barry looked around, a little startled to see Mr Pawlek approaching across the gravelled area in front of the church. But then most Poles were Catholics, so perhaps it wasn't that surprising to see the drill teacher at Mass.

He approached now, smiled at Barry and said, 'Good morning.'

'Good morning, sir.'

Mr Pawlek turned to Grandma and bowed formally, then held out his hand.

'Karl Pawlek, Madame.'

'Pleased to meet you, Mr Pawlek,' answered Grandma shaking hands. 'Peg Malone, Barry's grandmother. I've heard a lot about you.'

Mr Pawlek tilted his head a little playfully. 'Really? Not all bad, I hope?'

'No, no, no – nothing but good!'

'How flattering,' said the teacher with a grin. 'If only all my pupils were like Barry.'

'Oh now…' said Grandma with a high-pitched little laugh.

She beamed with pleasure, but Barry felt uncomfortable. Obviously he didn't look red-eyed, which was good. But it was embarrassing to be discussed like this, and he felt vaguely unsettled with how readily Grandma was responding to Mr Pawlek's charm.

'He's doing well at school. Very good at maths, according to his master,' said the Pole.

Barry hadn't realised that his master, Mr O'Brien, had been discussing him with the drill teacher.

'Takes after my Derek, if I say so myself,' said Grandma proudly.

'Ah yes, your son in the navy. He's doing well, I'm sure.'

'Oh yes, he's a Petty Officer now.'

'Really? You must miss him – so far away.'

'Yes,' answered Grandma, 'but he's good at writing. Sent me a lovely picture of Gibraltar for my birthday.'

Mr Pawlek raised an eyebrow. 'Gibraltar? That must be an interesting spot to be based.'

'Yes, though of course he's not really supposed to say where he is.'

'No, of course. Nice though that he's in touch.'

'Derek was always a good lad,' said Grandma.

'And Barry tells me his mother is working hard in Liverpool,' said Mr Pawlek.

'Ellen is a great girl.'

'Let's hope she can get over to visit.'

'Yes, she's trying to organise her holidays.'

'Good, good. A fine city, Liverpool,' added Mr Pawlek, 'when I first left Poland I worked there for a while.'

'Really?' said Grandma with interest.

'Yes, I lived in Allerton and commuted to work in Birkenhead. Where does your daughter-in-law have to travel to?'

Barry thought that Mr Pawlek was being a bit nosey, but Grandma answered readily.

'Out past Aintree. She gets a bus there and back. Great little worker, Ellen.'

'I'm sure she is,' agreed Mr Pawlek. 'Well, I mustn't keep you. Nice to have met you, Mrs Malone. Barry.'

'Sir.'

'Lovely meeting you, Mr Pawlek,' said Grandma.

The drill teacher nodded politely in farewell, then headed off across the churchyard.

'He's a proper gentleman,' said Grandma. 'You're lucky to have him, Barry.'

'Yes,' answered Barry, and he walked alongside his grandmother as they made for the churchyard gate. He said nothing more, knowing that Grandma was probably right. But still, just at the moment, somehow he didn't feel lucky.

Grace was shocked, even though she had tried to prepare herself. It was her first visit back to the North Strand since the night of the bombing, and now she and Ma were walking through their old neighbourhood. Dozens of houses had been demolished and damaged on the night of the raid, but more had since been razed to the ground because of their dangerous, bomb-damaged condition. And hundreds more homes couldn't be lived in until repairs had been carried out. The summer sun shone down onto streets that had been cleared of rubble by now, but Grace couldn't help but feel that the neighbourhood as she knew it was changed forever.

It had been a strange few days in general. Grace and Ma had been to a Mass for those who had died in the air raid, and the ceremony had been attended by the Taoiseach, Eamon de Valera, and other members of the government. The Army Band had played, and Grace had felt important to be present as a member of the North Strand community. At the same time she felt really sad about neighbours who had been killed, and a little guilty about enjoying the band and the sense of occasion.

On a brighter note, Uncle Freddie hadn't tried to get any friendlier with Ma, and had missed yesterday's trip to the Hollow in the Phoenix Park. He had been called in to work overtime as Dublin Corporation went flat out to finish its new housing scheme in Cabra, so that people displaced from the North Strand could be housed.

Grace wished that she and Ma could have had one of the new houses. For years they had had a joke between them – going back to when Grace was a toddler – that a fancy house near the strand in Sutton was 'Grace's house', and that she would live in it when she was grown up. Now she would have been delighted to take one of the more modest houses being finished in Cabra. Priority was given to larger families, however, and she and Ma would have to stay in Granddad's until Ma could find somewhere else.

Grace had enjoyed the trip to the Hollow with Granddad and Ma. Granddad had even treated her to a pink fizzy drink at the park entrance – though it still seemed a bit strange to hear a brass band playing jolly tunes, when only a week before so many people had been killed in the same city.

Now that they could see again the devastation of the North Strand the contrast seemed even more jarring, and Grace sensed that Ma was upset as they walked through the shattered neighbourhood. She squeezed her mother's hand and looked at her. 'Are you OK, Ma?'

'Yes…yes, I'm all right, love.'

Grace slipped her arm around her mother's waist as they walked along. It was the first time she ever felt responsible for her mother, and it was strange to have their normal roles reversed. They reached the door of Mrs Murray's house, an old friend and neighbour of Ma's, and they halted.

'I'll just pop in for a few minutes, Grace, you go and play with the girls,' said Ma, indicating three nearby girls who were using a piggy to play hopscotch on the pavement.

'OK,' answered Grace. Her two closest friends, Joan and Kathleen, had also lost their homes and were staying with relatives, but Grace knew the girls who were playing hopscotch and she greeted them easily.

'Hello, girls,' she said, approaching.

'Grace,' said the one who was throwing the piggy. 'Where are you living now?'

'Arbour Hill.'

The second girl raised an eyebrow. 'Where's Arbour Hill when it's at home?'

'It's near Stoneybatter.'

'Why did you move there?'

'It's where my grandda lives. I'm going to school there too, Ma says it's too far to be coming back here.'

'And what are the teachers like?'

'Same as here. Some are grand, some are a pain.'

'Any nice youngfellas?' asked the third girl.

'No, sure it's a girls' school.'

'I meant in Arbour Hill.

'Oh. No...no, I just got to know some of the girls,' answered Grace.

It was a lie, she realised immediately – she had made a friend in Barry. *Why had she hidden that?* Maybe it was because Barbara, the girl who had questioned her, was nosey and silly, and was always talking about boys. Grace didn't want her going on about herself and Barry and perhaps making fun of her new English friend.

She was a little surprised by her protectiveness, but though Barry certainly wasn't a boyfriend, she still thought of him as a friend. And he hadn't just left his *neighbourhood,* like her, he had left his *country*. So she would stand up for him if need be, or better still, keep his existence from silly busybodies like Barbara.

She took the piggy before the other girl could question her further, threw it accurately onto the far end of the chalked bed, then hopped confidently along the pavement in front of the bombed out houses of her old neighbourhood.

CHAPTER SIX

Barry felt the hairs rising on the back of his neck and he tensed himself, sensing danger. He was walking home from school, and lots of other boys were making their way along Brunswick Street, but that didn't guarantee safety.

McGrath and his friends, Nolan and Byrne, were walking slightly in front of him, and Barry had picked up on smirks and exchanged glances and he suspected that something was afoot involving him.

He knew that he shouldn't have antagonised McGrath earlier in the playground, but he hadn't been able to hold his tongue when the class bully had lectured the other boys.

'Every bleedin' foreigner in the country should be locked up!' McGrath had declared. 'Locked up or sent back where they came from!'

'Why's that, Shay?' asked Charlie Dawson.

'Because they could be spying on Ireland. My da says the Germans and the English both want Ireland as a base – so they have their spies here in case they invade.'

'And what are they spying on?' asked Charlie.

'Airfields, harbours, army barracks, places where landing craft can come ashore, places for dropping paratroops.'

'Right,' said Charlie, sounding impressed.

'We shouldn't put up with all these foreigners; they should all be rounded up!'

McGrath said it with venom and he looked directly at Barry, but Barry didn't respond.

'But how would you round them up?' asked Charlie. 'How would you know who they were?'

'Easy. You listen to them. And anyone who has an accent, you lock them up or kick them out.'

'Really?' said Barry, unable to hold back any longer. 'So it's Mountjoy Jail for Brother Fahy and his thick Kerry accent then?' he said sarcastically.

Several of the boys laughed, but McGrath's face darkened.

'Do you think the war is a joke, Malone?'

'No, I don't. But locking up anyone with an accent is.'

'A lot of Irish people died in the North Strand – and you're making jokes,' persisted McGrath. 'But you don't care, do you, you're not Irish.'

'My dad is Irish, my grandma is Irish, my cousins are Irish. Of course I care, but–'

'*But?* But what?!' demanded McGrath.

Barry answered calmly. 'The North Strand raid was awful. I know, more than anyone.'

'What's that supposed to mean?'

'I've been in raids, loads of them. But *one* plane bombed Dublin and it dropped *four* bombs. *Six hundred* planes raided Liverpool and dropped *thousands* of bombs. You don't know the first thing about air raids.'

McGrath didn't have a ready answer, and Barry sensed that the other boys had been influenced by his argument. Quitting while he was ahead, he turned on his heel and walked off, leaving McGrath looking a little foolish.

That had been this afternoon, but now, as Barry made his way home, he feared that McGrath was out to pay him back. They walked along Brunswick Street and approached the junction with Grangegorman. This was where McGrath, Nolan and Byrne turned off for Kirwan Street. If Barry could get past the corner he would be safe for another day. He didn't want to run in fear, but he picked up his pace a little and began to round McGrath and his group.

'Don't be in such a rush, Malone,' said McGrath, blocking his way.

The other two boys moved behind Barry, and he felt himself trapped, but tried not to show his anxiety.

'Nothing to say for yourself?' taunted McGrath. 'You'd loads of lip earlier.'

'Everything I said was true.'

'You're still a smart-aleck, English loudmouth. But we'll put manners on you!'

McGrath nodded, and Barry felt himself gripped from behind by Nolan and Byrne. McGrath moved quickly, scooping the lid off a nearby dustbin full of factory ash. He swiftly dipped the dustbin lid into the dirty grey ash then approached Barry, who struggled fiercely.

'Hold him tighter,' said McGrath, and he drew nearer, holding up the ash.

'No!' cried Barry, unable to escape as the bully held the bin lid above his head. McGrath was so close that Barry could smell sweat from him, then McGrath tipped the ash all over his head.

Barry spluttered, blinded by the ash, then he was roughly pushed and he lost his balance, falling against the factory wall. He heard laughter, and rubbed his eyes, clearing them of the fine ash that his school cap had only partially kept off his face.

He rose shakily to his feet and saw McGrath and his friends running away, laughing.

'Not so smart now!' McGrath called as he ran up the slope of Grangegorman.

Barry was aware that other people were staring at him. Humiliated and furious, he quickly brushed himself down, then continued unhappily on his way home.

Grace stepped carefully over the cow dung that littered Stoneybatter as she travelled home from school. The dung was a nuisance, but Grace thought it was a small price to pay for the fun of seeing cattle being herded by the drovers right past the door of the cake shop. Hundreds of cattle were kept in pens in the nearby cattle market, and Grace loved the excitement when they were herded down Manor Street and Stoneybatter by the drovers and their clever, barking dogs. She was slightly disappointed that so far she hadn't seen an animal run amok, but a big black cow with saliva running from its mouth had mounted the pavement and gone past the window of the cake shop, and Grace reckoned that that was the next best thing.

She crossed the thoroughfare now, making sure not to soil her shoes, and made for the junction of Stoneybatter and Arbour Hill. As she reached the corner she saw Barry, his schoolbag on his back, as he too returned from school.

'Barry!' she called in greeting.

'Grace,' he answered in a lacklustre voice.

Drawing closer, she realised that something was wrong. 'What happened?' she asked.

'Nothing.'

'Your cap, Barry' she said indicating the soiled school cap that he carried in his hand. 'And your hair is all dusty.'

Barry said nothing, and Grace felt concerned for him. She laid her hand gently on his arm. 'Who did this to you?'

Barry hesitated, then shrugged. 'Shay McGrath and his gang,' he said flatly. 'It's ashes from a bin.'

'Why did they do that?'

'McGrath doesn't like me.'

'And who's this Shay McGrath?'

'A boy in my class.'

Grace felt angry at this unknown boy. 'Has he done stuff like this before?' she asked.

'He's just said things till now.'

'You can't let him do this to you, Barry.'

'He has a gang.'

'Well, could you tackle him when he's on his own?'

'He's always with them, and…'

'What?' said Grace encouragingly.

Barry looked down and spoke quietly. 'Even if he wasn't, I don't think I could beat him. He's big and tough and…' Barry didn't finish the sentence but just shrugged dispiritedly.

'Tell your grandma then.'

'No.' said Barry. 'That would only make things worse.'

'How would it?'

'If she complained they'd say I was a squealer.'

'Let them!' said Grace angrily. 'That's what bullies count on, Barry, that people say nothing. Don't protect them.'

'I'm protecting myself.'

This wasn't how to deal with bullying, but before she could argue that he had to speak up for himself, Barry raised his hand to stop her.

'I don't want Grandma dragged into this. Promise you'll say nothing, Grace.'

Grace hesitated.

'Promise!'

'OK, I won't tell her.'

Barry looked at her piercingly.

'I promise,' repeated Grace, then Barry nodded in acceptance.

'Slip into our house first and we'll clean your cap and hair,' she said, 'you can't go in to your granny like that.'

'All right. And don't worry, I'll…I'll find a way to sort out McGrath.'

'OK,' said Grace and she fell into step beside him as they started walking up Arbour Hill, the air pungent with the smell from the piggery off Chicken Lane. Grace felt really sorry for Barry, though she knew he'd probably feel worse if she made that too obvious.

Was there something she could do to solve the problem? Ma always said that where there's a will there's a way. Was that just a saying though, or was it really true? She had to make it *be* true, she decided, then she continued on her way, her head spinning as she tried to come up with a solution.

CHAPTER SEVEN

'Great shot!' said Mr Pawlek.

'Thanks, sir,' answered Barry, pleased with the praise. He had scored a nice long-range goal in the schoolyard football game that had just broken up.

'I'd be proud to hit a shot like that myself,' said the drill teacher.

'Do they play much soccer in Poland, sir?' asked Barry.

'Yes, a good bit.'

'And what club do you support?'

'A local club from my city – you wouldn't have heard of them.'

'Which city is that, sir?'

'Danzig. Anyway, what I wanted to say is that you should try for the school Gaelic football team.'

Barry felt flattered. 'Really?'

'I know Gaelic football is different to soccer, but you have the ball skills. You should try for the team if you're still here in September.'

'Thanks, sir. But I don't know if I will be. It all depends on my mum.'

'Ah yes. Still busy making aeroplanes?'

'Yes, sir. But if she decides I'm staying here in Dublin, I'd love to get onto the Gaelic team.'

'Good. I'm not guaranteeing anything now – I'd have to talk

to Brother Hogan. But sport is a good way to impress your classmates.'

Barry wondered if Mr Pawlek had heard somehow of his problems with McGrath and his gang. They hadn't bothered him in the couple of days since the ash incident, but Barry suspected that Mr Pawlek was right about sport. Answering his classmates' questions about going to Liverpool's famous Anfield Stadium had already helped break the ice – and lots of the boys had been impressed when he had told of seeing Irish soccer star Jackie Hurley playing for Manchester United. If he could also get onto the school team that might offer further protection against the threat of bullying.

'If you want to get fit for the autumn, I'm running a summer sports camp this year,' said the teacher.

'Really? I'd love that, sir.' Then a thought struck Barry. 'I'd have to ask my grandma, though. Would she have to pay?'

'There's a small fee. I'm sure we can work something out.'

'Thanks, sir, that would be great.'

Mr Pawlek nodded, and Barry decided that things were looking up. Then he noticed Shay McGrath and his friends. They were standing behind the drill teacher and they were all making licking motions with their tongues. Barry ignored them and instead made his farewell to Mr Pawlek. He walked towards the classroom door, discouraged that the problem with McGrath clearly hadn't gone away. And while there might be hope for the future if he made it onto the school team, what was he going to do in the meantime?

Grace was eager to be off on the mission she had set herself, but she was afraid it might look suspicious if she didn't finish her tea. She sat at the table with Ma, Granddad and Uncle Freddie. She didn't want them enquiring about where she planned to go next, so she forced herself to have another slice of bread and not to appear rushed.

The bread today was discoloured due to poor quality flour. It made Grace wonder how Miss Kinsella so often managed to get top quality ingredients for the bakery. Outside of official rationing some people bartered and bought goods illegally on the black market. But Grace had grown to really like her card-playing, chain-smoking boss, and if Nellie Kinsella somehow got good quality supplies it wasn't Grace's place to question it.

Instead she now began spreading some of Ma's homemade gooseberry jam on the bread to make it taste a bit better.

'Smashin' jam, that,' said Freddie. 'Amn't I right, Grace?'

'Yes,' she answered unenthusiastically, not wanting to encourage her uncle when he played up to Ma like this.

Ma shrugged 'Sure anyone could make it.'

'Modesty will get you nowhere in this house, Nancy,' said Granddad with a grin. 'Take any compliments going.'

'Fair enough.'

'Gorgeous jam,' continued Freddie. 'Sure, look at Grace, laying it on with a trowel. Between that and trying the cakes in the shop, you'll be as fat as a fool, what?!'

Grace gave him a look, and Freddie raised his hands in defence. 'Only coddin', Grace, only coddin'.'

'You're not exactly fading away yourself!' said Granddad.

Freddie pointed at Ma. 'Blame this woman here. Ever since she came to stay we've been eating like kings!'

'Will you go way outta that, Freddie, 'deed and you haven't,' said Ma, but she said it with a smile.

How could she take any pleasure from Freddie's stupid flattery? Grace thought.

'So, what do you make of the British and the Free French landing in Syria?' asked Granddad.

Grace was relieved at the war becoming the topic of conversation and taking the focus off Freddie's embarrassing efforts to butter up Ma.

'They could wind up getting a right hiding in Syria,' Freddie said authoritatively. 'A right hiding'.

Grace felt like asking what he'd know about it – an electrician living in a neutral country – but instead she concentrated on finishing her bread and jam. Freddie started outlining what he would do if he was in command, and Grace decided that she couldn't take any more. 'That was lovely, thanks, Ma,' she said. 'Can I be excused please?'

Ma hesitated. 'Everyone isn't finished, Grace.'

'Ah, sure let the child go. She doesn't want to listen to Freddie talking guff,' said Granddad.

'Who's talking guff?'

'You are,' said Granddad, 'sure aren't you always?'

'All right, Grace,' said her mother before Freddie could begin his counter-attack. 'Be back by nine o'clock.'

'I will,' said Grace, rising from the table. 'See you later.' She headed for the door, trying not to show how anxious she was for the mission that lay ahead.

'God, my head is addled here,' said Grandma. 'What's a six-letter word meaning melodic?'

Barry was with her in the sunlit kitchen, Grandma in her favourite chair doing the newspaper crossword, while Barry sat at the table, writing a letter to his mother.

'A word for melodic? Eh...musical?' he suggested.

'No, that has seven letters. It has to have six, and the fifth letter is h.'

'Another word for melodic...' mused Barry. 'Eh...catchy?'

'Six letters, the fifth a h – yes!' cried Grandma triumphantly. 'How did I not get that?'

'I suppose we can't all be geniuses,' said Barry with a straight face.

Grandma laughed, and Barry smiled back at her, then watched as she happily filled in the answer, the evening paper propped up on her knees.

He had always been fond of his Irish grandmother, but since coming to stay in Dublin he had grown to know her better and his affection had deepened. But Grandma Peg had a gentle nature, and Barry felt that he couldn't burden her with the problem of his being bullied. He also felt that he couldn't ask her to pay for him to go to summer camp with Mr Pawlek. The drill teacher had said they would work out something on the fees, but Barry had no idea how well-off or otherwise Grandma was, and he didn't want to put her on the spot. Then again, the idea of the summer sports camp sounded great. And if he was still here in September he wanted to get on the school team, especially if it meant an end to bullying by McGrath.

There was only one answer – he had to ask Mum for the money. Would she think spending cash on that was foolish? And could she afford it? He knew that she was earning good money in the factory, but maybe she would have to save that to come to Dublin on holidays. Back in Liverpool she hadn't minded paying for piano lessons, however, and now he wasn't getting those, so perhaps she could use that money for Mr Pawlek's camp.?

He would have to sell the idea to her in his letter, and he thought about the Polish drill teacher and how he would describe him to Mum. Mr Pawlek was a good teacher, managing to be friendly yet still respected by the boys in school. He was certainly a bit nosey, what with all his questions about Mum and Dad, and where Mum worked in Liverpool, but Barry liked him. And besides, being nosey just meant that he was interested in people, and surely that was a good thing?

Barry put down his pen and thought for a moment. He had asked for all the news from Liverpool, and enquired about his friends. He had also asked Mum if she had been over to the Wirral Peninsula – a place she loved – and if she had had candy floss on the promenade at New Brighton this summer.

He had been at pains to keep the letter positive-sounding, and had told Mum nothing of his troubles in school. She was concerned enough about Dad, and there was no point in worrying her about something she couldn't deal with from Liverpool. So he would keep the tone of the letter happy, but would make it clear that he would really like to do the summer sports camp. His mind made up, he picked up the pen again and began writing, eager to make a good case.

'*Ice cream, a penny a lump, the more you eat, the more you jump!*'

It was a rhyme that Grace had never heard in the North Strand. She had to smile as a group of children sang it at the heavy-set woman who came out of a shop in Stoneybatter eating an ice cream.

Grace continued on her way, turning into Brunswick Street, then stopping outside a couple of tenement houses where hordes of children were playing street games. She approached a girl of about her own age who was swinging a friend on a rope tied to a lamppost.

'Can you tell me where I'd find Johnny Keogh?' she asked.

'That fella over there in the navy corduroys,' answered the girl.

'Thanks.'

Grace looked to the corner where a group of boys were playing a rough game of Red Rover Cross Over. Johnny Keogh was a stocky boy who carried himself with a confident air despite his clothes being a bit ragged. Grace could see at once that he was the leader of the group. She watched them for a moment, then heard the cry of *'All in all in, the game is broke up!'*

As all the boys returned to their starting point, she seized her opportunity and approached him.

'Johnny Keogh?'

He turned around and looked at Grace with a hint of aggression. 'Who's asking?'

'Grace Ryan. Can I talk to you?'

'You already are.'

'On your own. I don't want everyone to hear.'

Keogh looked hard at her, then his curiosity got the better of him. 'OK,' he answered, gesturing towards the corner of Stanley Street. Grace followed him around the corner, where he stopped and faced her.

'So, what do you want?'

'I want to ask you a question,' said Grace. 'Do you like cakes?'

Keogh looked at her suspiciously. 'What?'

'Do you like cakes?'

'Yeah, why?'

'But you don't get them often, do you?'

'What are you trying to make out?' said Keogh aggressively.

'Nothing,' answered Grace, raising her hands in a gesture of peace. 'I don't get them often either. Or I didn't before I started working in Kinsella's shop. But now I do. I sample bits and pieces, and I get two free tarts each week – they're gorgeous.'

'What are you telling me for?'

'You could have one of them. A whole rhubarb tart for yourself every week.'

Keogh looked at her with the air of someone who knew that nothing came for nothing. 'What would I have to do?' he said.

'It might mean a bit of fighting.'

'Yeah?'

'I'm told that you're the toughest kid in Brunner,' said Grace. 'That you're afraid of no-one in the school.'

'Who told you that?'

'What does it matter? Either it's true or it's not.'

'It's true.'

'Sure?'

'I've never backed down from anyone who wants his go!'

Grace nodded. 'I believe you.'

'So who do you want me to fight? And why?'

'I've an English friend called Barry Malone. He's really sound, but he's being bullied by Shay McGrath. Do you know him?'

'Yeah, I know him.'

'Could you frighten him enough to make him stop?'

Keogh looked at her with a wry smile on his lips. 'I could frighten anyone in that school,' he said simply.

'Make him stop and I'll give you a tart every week.'

'For how long?'

Grace considered for a moment. 'I'll give you one each week for a month.'

She didn't know how she would explain at home about having only one tart if Miss Kinsella mentioned to Granddad the perk of two free weekly tarts. But she would worry about that if she had to. Right now she had to win over Johnny Keogh. She looked at him, and could sense that he was tempted by the idea of a juicy rhubarb tart each week. *Time to close the deal.*

Grace spat on her hand, the way she had seen the drovers do at the cattle market, and she held her hand out to Keogh. 'A whole rhubarb tart every week. Have we got a deal?'

Keogh looked at her, his eyes calculating. Then he smiled briefly again, spat on his palm, and shook hands on their agreement.

CHAPTER EIGHT

Barry's mind was miles away as his class finished their drill routine with Mr Pawlek in the schoolyard. Today the summer air carried the mixed smells from the soap factory and the bakery, but Barry was oblivious to the oddly blended aromas.

The morning newspaper had carried a story regarding the German Army's successful occupation of the Mediterranean island of Crete. He wondered if Dad's ship had been involved in evacuating the British troops that had escaped from the island, and he wished, yet again, that his father was allowed to tell them where he was and what he was doing.

Barry's reverie was broken by Mr Pawlek calling for the attention of the class.

'Stand easy, boys,' he said, 'I've an announcement.'

Barry listened with his classmates, curious at what was to be revealed.

'I'm happy to say that I have the details of the school tour.'

There was a murmur of excitement, and now Barry was fully attentive. From the time he had arrived in his new school the other boys had been talking about this tour. Grandma had cleared his attendance with Mum, to Barry's delight, for not every pupil in the class could afford to go.

'We will be leaving the school at eight o'clock sharp on Thursday morning to get the train to Cork,' said Mr Pawlek. 'I'm told that all the money must be paid by the end of this week, and there'll be no refunds for anyone who misses the trip because he's late. We really *will* be leaving at eight. We should be back at the school at about nine-thirty that night.' He paused, then added smilingly, 'Oh, and I'm also told there'll be no homework for the next morning!'

The pupils cheered, and Barry joined in happily.

'All right, boys, dismissed,' said Mr Pawlek, then he took up his kitbag and headed off across the schoolyard.

Charley Dawson turned to Barry and grinned. 'Sounds good, doesn't it?'

'Great. I'm really looking forward to it.'

'Yeah, you can sit on Pawlek's knee, Malone!' said Shay McGrath.

McGrath's friends laughed, but Barry ignored it.

'The pair of youse should catch a ship in Cork while you're at it – and leave Ireland for the Irish,' added McGrath.

'My dad *is* Irish,' argued Barry.

'Pity he doesn't act it. My aul' fella is a real Irishman, not running off to be Winston bleedin' Churchill's lapdog.'

'My dad's no-one's lapdog!' snapped Barry.

'He's fighting for the English, isn't he?'

'Against the Nazis. So are fifty thousand other Irish. Are they all lapdogs too?'

'Yeah! And your aul' fella is the biggest lapdog of all!'

McGrath pushed Barry as he delivered the insult. Barry couldn't retreat this time. Despite his fear of the bigger boy, he pushed back, although he knew that it would probably lead to a beating. He saw McGrath smiling as though he were pleased that Barry had reacted. McGrath slowly moved forward until he was almost eyeball to eyeball with Barry, and the other boys circled around, relishing the prospect of a fight.

Barry clenched his fists, ready to defend himself. But before any blows were struck someone said, 'Back off, Muttonhead!' and McGrath was suddenly yanked backwards.

McGrath swung around in fury, but Barry saw that the boy who had man-handled him didn't look in the least concerned. He was Johnny Keogh, a stocky, rough-looking boy from 6C, the least academic of the classes. Barry had always kept well away from him, knowing his reputation as a lethal fighter and the toughest kid in school.

Despite his obvious anger, McGrath hesitated on seeing who his opponent was. Keogh looked coolly at McGrath. 'Want your go, Muttonhead?' he asked.

Nobody in Barry's class would have dared to call McGrath an insulting name, and Barry watched closely, amazed at this intervention, and curious to see how McGrath would react. To his surprise, McGrath said nothing. The other boy approached him menacingly, just as McGrath had done to Barry.

'Go on. Try it if you're so keen for a scrap.'

Keogh wasn't any bigger than McGrath but he was heavily built and there was an unmistakable air of menace about him. McGrath was clearly affected by it and he made no response.

The other boy nodded. 'Didn't think so,' he said.

McGrath stared hard back at him but still said nothing.

'So you don't like the English,' said Keogh. 'That's a pity. 'Cause if you even look crooked at the English kid here, I'll beat you from one end of the yard to the other.'

Barry could hardly believe his ears. *How had Keogh heard about his troubles with McGrath? And why was he taking his side?* McGrath looked over at him now, real hatred in his eyes.

'Don't look at him, Muttonhead, look at me,' ordered Keogh, and McGrath turned back to him.

'I'm only going to tell you this once,' continued Keogh. 'If I've to come back, you'll end up in a bed in the Richmond.'

The Richmond was the hospital across the road from the school, and rumour had it that a boy from a gang in Thomas Street had been laid up there for a week after a fight with Keogh. McGrath made no answer to the threat, and Keogh casually reached out, pushed McGrath in the chest and was already walking away by the time McGrath regained his balance.

Barry stood there, his mind spinning. *Why had he been protected by somone who had never even looked at him before now*? He couldn't figure it out, but maybe his prayers had been answered. He knew that he shouldn't antagonise McGrath, but their eyes met now, and Barry couldn't help himself. He smiled at McGrath, gave him a wink, then turned and walked casually towards the classroom door.

CHAPTER NINE

Grace was really worried, but she kept her voice cheerful as she chatted to her boss in the oven-warmed cake shop. It was Saturday, normally a busy day, but Nellie Kinsella was leaving Grace alone in the shop for the afternoon. The older woman was meeting a bridge friend who was arriving by train in Amiens Street station, and she drew heavily on her cigarette as she prepared to leave. Grace normally disliked the smell of cigarettes, but today she hardly noticed, so distracted was she.

'Are you all right, Grace?' asked the shop owner, tilting her head to one side and looking Grace in the eye.

'Yes, Miss Kinsella, I'm fine.'

'Don't worry. You're well up to running the place, even on a Saturday. I've every confidence, or I wouldn't leave you.'

'Thanks,' said Grace, trying for a smile. 'I'm sure it'll be grand.'

'Good,' said Nellie smiling back at her 'And here – treat yourself to a jam tart.'

'Thanks, Miss Kinsella.'

'Sure we'll be a long time dead, that's what I always say!'

Grace forced another smile. 'I suppose we will.'

'I'll be back to lock up at six. See you then.'

'Bye.'

Graced watched as Nellie made for the door. Her eyes followed the tall angular frame of her boss as she strode off towards Stoney-batter, then Grace served several customers before there was a lull again and she was left alone with her thoughts.

She had told Nellie that she was fine, but in fact she was terrified that she was going to lose her job. The wages from working part-time in the cake shop weren't huge, but every penny counted. Ma worked hard in a shirt factory in town, but money was always scarce, and her mother had had to find cash to buy replacement clothes after they lost all their possessions in the bombing. Ma was good at getting a bargain and had got secondhand clothes at the best possible price in the Daisy Market. It was an expense Ma could have done without, however, so Grace's wages from the cake shop were very welcome. And now they would be stopped if Miss Kinsella sacked her.

Was there any way she could get around the problem? But however hard she racked her brains she couldn't see a way out of her predicament. There was a shortfall in the till of five shillings, and Nellie Kinsella would discover it when she locked up at six and tried to balance the cash. Two half crowns were missing from the cash register, stolen that morning during the half hour when Nellie had gone to do her grocery shopping, leaving Grace alone in the cake shop.

Although Grace had an idea of who had taken the money, it would be impossible to prove it. Which meant that Miss Kinsella would think that Grace had stolen the money herself, or that she had been careless enough to let somone else take it. Either way it was a disaster. She looked at the clock on the wall. One o'clock. She had five hours to come up with a solution. And no idea where to start.

* * *

Barry was delighted with himself as he walked down Arbour Hill. He had heard the saying that good things come in threes, and this week it had been true. First there had been the incident when Johnny Keogh had challenged Shay McGrath. Barry still had no idea why Keogh had done it, but whatever the reason, it had worked, and McGrath hadn't come near him over the last two days. Then yesterday after school, Charlie Dawson had introduced him to some boys who lived near him on Norseman Place, and they had all played football together. The boys were going to play again later this afternoon, and Barry had been invited to that also. And today a letter had come from his mother in the Saturday morning post.

It was a cheery letter that gave lots of news from Liverpool, and she had heard from Dad, who had written to say he was safe and well on his ship. His mother had agreed to thinking about sending him to the summer camp next month, and meanwhile she had included a ten shilling note – enough to cover the cost of the school tour and still have three whole shillings left to spend.

He reached the end of Arbour Hill and turned into Stoneybatter, smiling as he remembered a cheeky piece of Liverpool humour that Mum had also included in the letter. It seemed that an umbrella shop in Clayton Square had been bombed by the Germans, and a sign had been put up saying, 'Damaged by Adolf Hitler and Company. Repairs by Tysons.' It was the kind of humorous, never-say-die response that made him proud of his hometown, and he crossed Stoneybatter and made for Kinsella's cake shop in good spirits.

Barry looked through the window and saw that Grace was behind the counter. He hadn't seen her for several days and he entered the shop and greeted her brightly.

'Grace!'

'Barry,' she answered.

'I've great news,' he said.

'Yeah?'

'Remember that bully I told you about, Shay McGrath? Well, he got a taste of his own medicine, and now he's leaving me alone.'

'Good.'

'He was told to back off by a really tough lad called Johnny Keogh.'

'Yeah, I know him,' said Grace.

Barry looked at her in surprise. 'You do?'

Grace hesitated, then sighed. 'I wasn't sure whether to tell you, but there's no point lying.'

'About what?'

'I got Keogh to do it.'

'What?!'

'I found out who was the toughest kid around, and I got him to threaten McGrath.'

'I don't need you fighting my battles, Grace.'

'What, you'd rather be bullied?'

'No. But–'

'But what?'

Barry tried to come up with an answer, but he couldn't. He knew that on his own against McGrath and his gang he couldn't have won. But it still hurt his pride that a girl had had to come to his aid.

'You're lucky I was able to persuade him,' Grace said.

'How did you?'

'Every week I get two free tarts here. I promised one of them each week to Keogh.'

Barry was taken aback. He realised how far Grace had gone on his behalf and suddenly he felt ashamed of how he had responded.

'Sorry, Grace. I...I didn't mean to sound...that was really decent.'

'It's all right, I hate bullies.'

'Even so, giving away half your stuff for me....'

'Forget it,' said Grace dismissively.

Barry took in her glum face and he felt even worse. 'I don't blame you being annoyed at me,' he said.

'It's not that.'

He looked at her again, realising that she seemed more downbeat than he had ever seen her before. 'What's wrong then?'

'I think I'm going to lose my job.'

'Why?'

'There's five shillings missing from the till. When Miss Kinsella comes back this evening she'll find out.'

'Where's the money gone?' asked Barry.

'Three kids came in here this morning when I was on my own for a bit. I had to go into the back to get loaves that had just come out of the oven. I think they must have taken the money out of the till.'

'Would you not have heard them?'

'They were singing and messing and making noise. It was probably to cover the sound of the till being opened.'

'That's awful. Do you know who they were?'

'I don't know their names, but I've seen them around.'

'Could you point them out to Miss Kinsella?'

'I can't accuse them when I've no proof.'

'Right,' said Barry thoughtfully. 'And you're certain it's not just a mistake, that the money is really gone?'

Grace nodded. 'There were two half-crowns in the till. They're both missing.'

'Funny that they didn't steal more than five shillings.'

'I thought about that,' said Grace. 'Maybe they felt five shillings wouldn't be noticed during the day, but I'd still get into big trouble when Miss Kinsella did the cash.'

'Why would they want to get you into trouble?'

'One of them was a boy with yellow buck teeth.'

' "Buck' Nolan?' said Barry.

'Is that what they call him? Anyway I remembered you telling me that one of McGrath's gang had buck teeth. So I thought maybe they did this 'cause I helped you.'

'But how would they know that you'd helped me?'

'Keogh might have said something,' answered Grace. 'Or he might have been seen when I gave him the tart. Or they might have heard that I'd gone looking for Johnny Keogh last week.'

Barry considered this. 'It mightn't have anything to do with Keogh at all. Though I suppose it is a bit of a coincidence.'

'It doesn't matter,' said Grace. 'I haven't an ounce of proof, so it's all the one.'

'And when is Miss Kinsella coming back?'

'We close at six. She'll be back to do the cash then.'

'Supposing you didn't tell her? Could you explain all this to your mum? If she gave you five shillings you could put it in the till and your boss needn't know.'

'I can't ask Ma. She's spent every penny she has getting us clothes.'

'What about your granddad or your uncle, then?'

Grace shook her head. 'We're already staying in their house and eating their food. I can't ask for money as well.'

Barry thought of the ten shillings his mother had sent him to cover the school tour. If he gave Grace the missing five shillings it would save her job. But then he wouldn't have enough to pay the seven shillings for the tour to Cork. *How could he possibly explain that to Mum?* And he had been really looking forward to the trip, especially now that he could relax with his classmates without McGrath picking on him. But then again, if it wasn't for Grace, McGrath would *still* be picking on him.

He bit his lip, trying to find an answer to his dilemma.

'Anyway, can I get you something?' asked Grace.

This was letting him off the hook, he realised. Grace was accepting that the situation was her problem, and if he gave his order now for Grandma's Saturday treat, the conversation would move on.

'Barry?'

'Eh, two rock buns and two jam slices, please,' he said.

'OK,' she said, reaching for a paper wrapper.

Barry watched her preparing to fill his order, then suddenly he made his mind up.

'Forget the cakes for now,' he said. 'I got ten bob from England this morning – take the five you need out of that.'

Grace stopped what she was doing and looked at him in amazement. 'I ...I can't do that, Barry,' she said.

Barry sensed that Grace might be too proud to accept what seemed like charity. But now that he had decided that he wanted to help, he racked his brains for a way that would allow her to accept.

'Look at it this way. You did me a good turn, and now I'm doing you one. But it's not just that. If you don't keep your job, there'll be no tarts to pay off Johnny Keogh. And if Keogh isn't on our side McGrath will come after me again. So it's best for both of us if you keep your job. OK?'

'I...I don't know what to say.'

Barry grinned. 'Just say "Thank you, Barry",' he said in a funny voice. For the first time since entering the shop he saw a smile on Grace's lips. 'We're in this together, Grace. They thought they were so smart, but this way we beat them. All right?'

Grace's smile broadened, and she nodded. 'All right!'

Barry grinned back at her, though he realised that in solving Grace's problem he had created a problem for himself. But even if he couldn't raise the money for the school tour, even if he got into trouble with Mum, he had done the right thing.

'OK,' he said cheerfully, 'now that that's settled, let's have the two jammiest jam slices in the shop.'

'Coming up!'

CHAPTER TEN

Grace wrinkled her nose in distaste as the slop cart went past. After nearly three weeks she was settling into life in Arbour Hill, but she still hated the smell of the nearby piggery, to which the slop man was guiding his foul-smelling, donkey-driven cart full of waste food for the pigs. The other children with whom Grace was playing didn't seem to notice, and Grace wondered how long you had to live close to a piggery before you got used to the smell. It probably took months, and she hoped that herself and Ma would have found somewhere else to live by then.

Meanwhile, she had to adapt. Her two closest friends, Joan and Kathleen, had also lost their homes in the North Strand, and it made Grace sad when she thought that because of the bombing they were all split up – maybe forever.

Grace had become friendly with May Bennett, a perky girl who lived behind her in Viking Place, and now she was with May and a group of boys and girls who were starting to organise a game of Kick the Can. May was arguing with Whacker Wallace about who would pick the teams. Grace found the boy silly and irritating, and now he was trying to boss May.

'I'm picking one team and Micksy's picking the other,' he said, indicating his friend, a heavy-set, placid looking boy.

'You must be joking,' said May. 'We're playing boys and girls together, so it's only fair a girl picks one team.'

'Says who?'

'Says me!' said May. 'You don't own the game, Whacker Wallace!'

Grace half listened as the argument continued, but out of the corner of her eye she saw Barry making his way up the road. He was with a blond-haired boy and they carried a football. Grace waved over to him, and Barry waved back as the two boys walked together in the direction of Norseman Place.

'What's the story with your man there?' asked Whacker, having seen Grace waving.

'That's Barry Malone,' she answered.

'Yeah, I heard about him. He's English and stuck up,' said Whacker.

'He's not a bit stuck up,' argued Grace.

'I heard his granny spoils him, and he has this weird English accent.'

'Of course he has an English accent, he comes from England,' said Grace.

Whacker pointed at Grace. 'Listen to your woman here. Are you his mot or something?'

'No.'

'You must be!'

'Don't mind him, Grace,' said May.

'*He's not stuck up – he's lovely!*' said Whacker, imitating Grace in a silly, high-pitched accent.

Some of the others laughed, and Grace sensed that as the new girl this was a kind of test for her. If she let someone like Whacker make fun of her then everyone else might think she was a pushover. And besides, Barry had proven to be a really loyal friend – she couldn't let this boy make little of him.

'Do you know what I'm going to tell you, Whacker?' she said, moving closer to him.

'What?'

'You're really smart, aren't you? One more wit – and you'd be a half wit!' It was a smart answer that she had learnt at the North Strand, but she saw that these kids had never heard it before, because there was a burst of laughter.

'That's telling you, Whacker Wallace!' said May. 'Now are you going to stand there with your mouth open like a fish, or are you going to pick one team while I pick the other?'

'All right!' said the boy in disgust. 'But I'm having first pick,' he insisted, in what Grace reckoned was an attempt to save some face.

Everyone gathered round as the sides began to be picked. Grace looked up the road at Barry's retreating form. She was glad that he had friends to play football with, and glad too that she had stood up for him. Most of all though she was glad to have a friend who had been willing to sacrifice so much of his own money to save her job. And if she had to spend the summer living with Granddad and Uncle Freddie, and without her old friends Joan and Kathleen, then it mightn't be so bad if she could share some of it with Barry Malone.

'I pick Grace!' said May, breaking her reverie. 'Come on, Grace!'

'OK,' she answered, then she turned and happily joined her team for Kick the Can.

Barry felt excited as the countryside whistled by outside the train window. He was sitting opposite an animated Charlie Dawson, and the rest of the sunlit carriage was full of other excited schoolboys taking part in the sixth class school tour to Cobh in County Cork. The boys' high spirits were infectious, and Barry was enjoying every minute of the fun, all the more so since it had looked at one stage like he wouldn't be able to make the tour.

When he had given the five shillings to Grace it had left him with a shortfall of two shillings. Grandma, however, gave him sixpence pocket money each Sunday – one week of which he had already saved – which meant that he was only a shilling short of the required seven shillings. And in a flash of inspiration he had decided to do a salvage drive around all the houses off Arbour Hill to raise the money.

Salvage drives had been popular in wartime Liverpool – *Saucepans for Spitfires* was the name they gave to one where old metal items were recycled to make fighter planes – but other items were collected too, and there was a ready market for rags, wool, bottles, jam jars and waste paper. Barry had worked hard collecting sacks full of old newspapers and crates of sticky beer bottles and jam jars that he brought to the gloomy warehouse of a scrap merchant on

Chicken Lane. It had been worth all the effort, and now he even had a few pence left over to spend on today's excursion.

Everyone in the class wasn't as lucky, and several boys whose fathers were out of work couldn't afford the trip. One of these was Shay McGrath, and Barry had discovered that McGrath's labourer father had been out of work for several months now. Barry had felt sorry for the other boys who were missing the trip, but it was a relief that McGrath was missing. The bullying had stopped since the magical day when Johnny Keogh had intervened, but it was obvious that McGrath still didn't like him, so the trip would be more relaxed in McGrath's absence.

The train sped on through the summer countryside, the fields outside the window a blur of green, occasionally masked by the thick, black smoke spewed out by the massive steam locomotive that pulled the train. Brother Hogan and Mr Pawlek were sitting together at the end of the carriage, but their demeanour was more easy-going than when in school, and the boys were taking advantage of the holiday atmosphere.

Suddenly Charlie clutched his stomach as though in pain. Barry looked at him anxiously, then realised it was a gag when Charlie cried out, ' "*I've a pain in me belly!*", *said Dr Kelly*.'

The rest of the boys shouted out in unison. ' "*Rub it with oil!*" *said Doctor Doyle*.'

Charlie jumped up as though cured. ' "*A very good cure!*", *said Doctor Moore*,' he cried.

Barry had never heard the rhyme before and he laughed heartily, entertained by Charlie's performance. He sat back contentedly, delighted to be off school, and sensing that this might be his best day since coming to Ireland.

* * *

The sun shone brightly, bathing Cobh in warm golden light. Barry walked along the waterfront, the waves in the harbour sparkling in the sunlight. High above him on the hill, Cobh cathedral seemed to soar up into the clear blue sky, while at ground level the curve of the bay provided a fine natural harbour. He could see where the transatlantic liners docked, while further west along the waterfront stood Haulbowline Island, headquarters of the Irish Navy.

Barry had been told that the Irish navy was small – *tiny* when compared to Britain's Royal Navy – but as the son of a serving seaman he was curious to see the main Irish naval base. The school tour had allowed the boys some free time, and after Barry and his classmates had visited the amusements at the eastern end of Cobh, Barry had chosen to walk back towards the western end. Many of the boys had gone on trips in rowing boats, but Barry had explained his interest in the navy and he headed off along the seafront towards Haulbowline.

He could feel the heat of the sun on his shoulders and he breathed in deeply, savouring the salty tang of the sea air. The waterfront was busy with people making their way to and from the nearby railway station, but Barry strolled at a leisurely pace, enjoying the sense of being on holiday.

He carried on until he was opposite the small outcrop known as Rocky Island, then he stopped and looked out across the water towards Haulbowline Island. He could make out the shape of a couple of grey naval vessels and he wondered what they were. Too small for destroyers, he thought, perhaps they were corvettes. He would have liked a closer look, but the naval base was off limits to civilians, and in any case it could only be reached by boat.

Barry continued gazing across the water, wondering what it must be like to serve in the Irish navy. Being neutral must be really odd. Particularly when on your doorstep in the Atlantic a life and death struggle was going on between the German U-boats and the Royal Navy convoys that brought vital supplies to Britain.

Of course, if Ireland had fought against Germany – or even allowed the Royal Navy to use its ports – then Irish cities would have been bombed by the dreaded *Luftwaffe*. And with Ireland having virtually no air force that would have meant the principal Irish cities being reduced to ruins. But though Barry could see why a small country like Ireland remained neutral, he also understood the frustration of people in England, who fumed about Ireland refusing to help protect the Atlantic convoys, while accepting some of the vital supplies that they carried.

It was a tricky situation, and he decided that a sunny day like this wasn't the time to worry about it. He was about to move off when out of the corner of his eye he caught a glimpse of a familiar shape. It wasn't someone he had expected to see here, and he looked again, surprised to confirm his first impression. The man who had caught his eye was Mr Pawlek. *What on earth was he doing on his own here, instead of being with the other teachers*?

Just then Barry saw the drill teacher raise a camera to his eye and quickly snap off a photograph. Barry was well out of his line of vision, and none of the other people who were coming and going paid much notice to the respectably dressed man looking out across the harbour. Fascinated, Barry watched him intently. There had been something furtive in the quick way he had taken the picture, and now Mr Pawlek moved a little further along the waterfront. Barry remained where he was but watched the teacher's every move. Mr Pawlek was still looking across the water towards Haulbowline, and after a moment he once more raised a small camera to his eye. While his general demeanour seemed casual, there was something slightly strange about the very quick way he snapped off another picture, then slipped the camera into the pocket of his jacket.

Barry stood unmoving but he felt the hairs stand up on his neck, a sixth sense telling him something was wrong here. *Why would a drill teacher want to take sly pictures of a naval base?* Barry had seen enough warning posters in Liverpool to know that this was the kind of thing done by spies. But Mr Pawlek being a spy seemed ridiculous. Barry tried to tell himself that he was being dramatic, that his over-active imagination was running away with him. Yet his instincts insisted that something wasn't right.

He watched as Mr Pawlek turned and made his way back along

the waterfront toward the centre of Cobh. Barry stood well back, out of the teacher's line of sight, but followed his progress as he walked away briskly.

Could he really be spying? Mr Pawlek was Polish, and Poland wasn't at war with Ireland, so that hardly made sense. *Unless, of course, he was lying*. Germany was right beside Poland. Supposing he was German, but pretending to be Polish? His English was excellent, and Barry couldn't have told the difference between a German and Polish accent. And a German agent might well be interested in Ireland's naval headquarters – especially if the Nazis decided to invade Ireland, which was still a fear of the Irish Government.

Barry thought too of all the innocent-seeming questions that Mr Pawlek had asked him: about where his father's ship was based, and where his mother's aircraft factory was situated in Liverpool. Wasn't that exactly the kind of information a spy gathered?

Mr Pawlek, enemy agent...in one way the idea was exciting. But mostly it was scary to think that he might be dealing with a Nazi, knowing how ruthless they were. Barry stood gazing over the water, the summer sun forgotten now as a tiny chill ran up his spine.

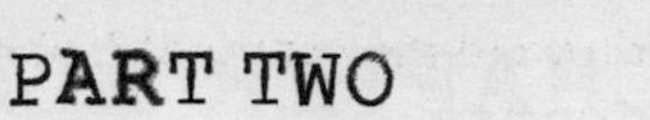

PART TWO

SUSPICIONS

CHAPTER ELEVEN

Grace hated doing homework, especially on bright summer evenings like this. Just one more week and school would be over, with the holidays stretching out before her. She had slotted in well at her new school in Stanhope Street, but she definitely wouldn't be sorry when the term ended.

Now that she had finished tea, Grace was sitting in a corner of the kitchen going over her spellings. Granddad was lighting his pipe, Uncle Freddie was reading the newspaper and Ma was doing her trick with the carrots – though Grace wished that she wouldn't.

Grace didn't want to hurt Ma's feelings, so she never complained about the taste when her mother grated carrots, baked the gratings in the oven, and then used the blackened results as 'tea leaves'. Ma mixed them with regular leaves to stretch out the supply of rationed tea, and sometimes when supplies were really short the carrot 'tea leaves' alone were used.

Ma was doing her best to keep everyone in the house happy. But Grace knew that she was trying to find somewhere else she could afford to rent, despite Granddad saying that they were welcome to stay as long as they liked.

'Your man Churchill takes the biscuit!' said Uncle Freddie, putting down his newspaper and shaking his head.

'What ails you now?' asked Granddad, puffing contentedly on his pipe.

'He's going on about freedom and keeping the Nazis at bay,' said Freddie.

'Well, in fairness, Freddie, isn't he doing just that?' answered Ma.

'Good woman, yourself, Nancy!' said Granddad with a chuckle.

Grace was pleased that Ma had disagreed with her uncle. When Freddie buttered Ma up she found it embarrassing, especially when Ma didn't dismiss his flattery outright.

'He's keeping the Nazis at bay,' argued Freddie, 'but the only freedom he cares about is England's.'

'How do you know what he cares about?' asked Granddad.

'From what he allowed. Didn't the Royal Navy pursue the German ship *Altmark* into a Norwegian fjord? They violated Norwegian waters – and the next thing you know the Nazis decided Norway wasn't really neutral, and invaded the country.'

'I didn't realise that,' said Ma.

'And Churchill has his beady eyes on our ports,' insisted Freddie.

'Are you saying Churchill's going to invade us?' said Granddad.

Despite normally dismissing most of what Uncle Freddie said, Grace couldn't help but be interested this time, and she put down her spelling book.

'Maybe not *now*, because we've raised an army, and he knows we'd fight him tooth and nail,' answered Freddie.

'So if he's not going to invade us, and he's resisting the Nazis, what's the problem?' said Granddad.

'The problem is we've spent a fortune we don't have expanding the army. That's money that could be spent on housing or schools.'

'There is that,' agreed Ma, who had strong views about the poor housing that so many people in Dublin had to endure.

'The bigger army is also to fight the Germans if they invaded,' argued Granddad, 'it's not just Churchill.'

'Maybe,' said Freddie, 'but this thing of Winston Churchill as some kind of saint, it's a load of…' Uncle Freddie stopped himself, though Grace wished he had let slip the rude word that he obviously wanted to use.

'It's a load of rubbish,' said Freddie.

Her uncle went back to his newspaper, and Grace picked up her spelling book again. She was meeting Barry later on and now she was really looking forward to it. Barry hero-worshipped the British Prime Minister, Mr Churchill, and now she had something with which to challenge him playfully. She returned to the spellings, eager to finish her homework and meet up with her friend.

Barry strode happily out the garden gate, the sweet smell of roses hanging in the air. Yesterday's school tour had been brilliant, and Barry was really glad he had managed to raise the money to go on it. In the relaxed atmosphere of the tour – and with Shay McGrath absent – he had gotten on well with his classmates and felt much more like one of the group. After visiting Cobh, they had all had high tea in a hotel in Cork, and there had been a great sing-song on the train coming home. Looking back, it had definitely been his happiest day since leaving Liverpool six weeks previously.

The only niggling thing had been the strange behaviour of Mr Pawlek in Cobh. Mum had always said Barry had a vivid imagination, and he had tried to convince himself that he was getting carried away in thinking of the drill teacher as a spy. But try as he might, he couldn't shake off the feeling that Mr Pawlek was up to something.

He hadn't shared his suspicions with any of the other boys in his class, not wanting to risk his recent acceptance by leaving himself open to ridicule. But he needed to tell someone, and he was looking forward to hearing Grace's opinion this evening.

They had arranged to meet after tea, and Barry reached her door and knocked, slightly nervous now that the time had come to share his secret. The door swung open, and Grace greeted him smilingly.

'Barry, come on in,' she said, 'we've a new record I want you to hear.'

'Great,' said Barry, stepping inside and following Grace into the front parlour. 'What is it?'

' "Blueberry Hill", by Gene Autry. Uncle Freddie got it in town.'

'That's a great song,' said Barry. 'I didn't think it would be your uncle's style.'

'He's not always an eejit,' said Grace, who had stopped before reaching the gramophone. She looked at Barry with a hint of playfulness. 'In fact, now and again he says something that's smart.'

'Like what?'

'Well, he says your Mr Churchill isn't the saint you think he is.'

'I never said he was a saint,' said Barry.

'You think he's great, though.'

'He *is* great. When Poland fell, and Belgium, and Holland and France, he still stood up to the Nazis. Even when England was the only country left, he wasn't afraid of them.'

'Uncle Freddie says he only cares about England – that he doesn't care about other people's rights.'

'Well it's easy for your uncle, isn't it?' said Barry, feeling irritated at Freddie.

'How is it?' asked Grace.

'*My* uncle is half starved in a Nazi prison camp. *Your* uncle is sitting on his backside in Dublin.'

'Why shouldn't he?' challenged Grace. 'Ireland is neutral.'

'Other Irishmen aren't neutral. My dad isn't. And he says there're loads of Irish fighting in the Royal Navy – and the RAF and the British Army.'

'That doesn't mean Uncle Freddie has to. He's entitled to his opinion.'

'Yeah, your uncle's spouting his opinions, while–'

'He's not *spouting*!'

'He is! But my uncle George *fought* for his, and ended up in a prison camp.'

'Well good for him!' retorted Grace.

Barry was shocked. He thought of his favourite uncle and all that he had suffered since his capture, then he looked Grace in the eye. 'Good for him? A prisoner of the Nazis – and you say "good for him"?'

'I don't...I didn't really mean it like that. It's just...'

'Just forget it, OK?' said Barry. He wasn't in the mood now to hear Gene Autry singing 'Blueberry Hill'. And he certainly wasn't going to reveal his suspicions about Mr Pawlek. 'I'll see you, Grace,' he said, and before there could be any more argument, he turned away and walked out of the room.

CHAPTER TWELVE

'Do you want to keep our deal going a bit longer?' asked Johnny Keogh as he took the rhubarb tart from Grace at the corner of Brunswick Street. The cake shop had just closed after a busy Saturday, and Grace was a little tired, but she looked at Keogh warily. So far they had both kept their parts of the bargain, and there had been no more bullying from Shay McGrath. But a boy as tough as Johnny Keogh had to be handled carefully.

'How do you mean?' she asked him.

'School finishes next week, so I'm due one more tart. But if you give me a couple more I'll make sure that there's no problem over the summer, even after school closes.'

Grace looked him in the eye, but Keogh stared back unblinkingly. *Was there a threat here? Was he subtly suggesting that if she didn't extend the deal then he would withdraw his protection? Perhaps even tell Shay McGrath that Barry was no longer protected, to force her to hire him again?* Grace felt bad enough after last night's row with Barry over his uncle. She couldn't let him be bullied again. But she didn't want Keogh taking advantage of her either.

'That's not the deal we had,' she said.

'You wanted your mate to be OK in school, and now he is. But Shay McGrath only lives in Kirwan Street cottages. He could easily bump into your friend over the summer, and McGrath might feel he's not protected now school's over.'

Grace kept her expression calm even though she felt annoyed. She was sure now that Keogh *was* subtly issuing a threat.

'I wouldn't say that Barry is all that likely to bump into McGrath,' she said. 'And even if he does, I'm sure McGrath is still afraid of you.'

Keogh went to speak, but Grace raised her hand, stopping him. 'But just to be sure, I'll tell you what I'll do,' she continued. 'I'll give you one extra week, to make certain there's no trouble over the summer.'

She could see that Keogh was weighing this up and she spoke again. 'Don't push your luck, you're getting an extra tart without having to do anything. OK?'

Keogh held her gaze, then gave a wry grin. 'OK.'

'Right, see you next week,' said Grace, then she turned and made off towards home. She crossed the busy thoroughfare of Stoneybatter, her mind distracted as she skipped between the sour smelling slop man's cart and a horse drawn milk float from the Lucan Dairy. Reaching Arbour Hill, she started up the incline and slowed down, trying to marshal her thoughts. All day long she had been thinking about the incident with Barry, and she wanted to make peace with him. But he had been annoyed by her remark about his uncle in the prison camp, and she wasn't sure how he would respond. *Only one way to find out,* she decided as she came to the terrace of houses where both their grandparents lived. She passed her own door, and the monkey puzzle tree that Freddie had planted in the small front garden, then she reached the gate at Barry's house and paused. She stood there a moment gathering her nerve, then swung open the gate, crossed to the front door and knocked.

After a moment Barry's grandma opened the door.

'Ah, Grace, come on in,' she said. 'Barry, Grace is here!' she called behind her.

Grace stepped in, hoping that Barry wouldn't still be angry.

'I'm just polishing the floor, love. Step into the front room there and I'll send him in to you.'

'Thanks very much,' said Grace, then she went into the parlour.

She heard the sound of approaching footsteps, and Barry came into the room.

'Hello, Barry,' she said.

'Grace,' he replied in a non-committal tone.

'Look, I'm sorry about last night. I didn't mean it to sound like it did.'

'Right.'

'I got you this,' continued Grace, placing a paper bag on the table. 'The jammiest jam slice in the shop!'

Barry's face creased into a smile, and Grace felt relieved. 'Pax?' she said.

'OK,' he answered.

'I really didn't mean to insult your uncle.'

'I know,' said Barry. 'Maybe...maybe I was a bit touchy.'

'Friends then?'

'Yeah, friends.'

'And I hope your Uncle George gets out safely, I really do.'

'Me too,' said Barry. 'He's my favourite uncle.'

'Yeah? What's he like?'

'Great fun. He's a delivery driver for Lewis's, the big store, and he taught me how to drive.'

'Really?'

'Yeah. He loves driving, says everyone should know how.'

'Where did he teach you?'

'On a quiet road down by the docks.'

'How long did that take?'

'A few weeks. He kept at it till I got good.'

'Brilliant.'

'Yeah, I like being with him. He's actually one of my first memories.'

'Oh? What was the memory?'

'We were at the Empire Theatre in Liverpool. He'd brought me to a show called "Mr Whittington". There were songs in it, and it was funny,' said Barry fondly, 'and when we came outside Lime Street was all cold and frosty. And Uncle George wrapped me up inside his overcoat. And I was trying to walk to the bus stop, and his feet and my feet were inside the coat and we were laughing.'

'Sounds nice.'

'It was.'

Grace could see that Barry looked a little wistful, so she decided to change the subject. 'Talking of good memories, how was the school tour?'

'Great. We went to Cobh. Do you know it?'

'I know of it,' said Grace. 'Our teacher said it was the last port the *Titanic* visited. But I've never been.'

'It's where the Irish navy has its headquarters. And...'

Barry hesitated, and Grace looked at him enquiringly. 'What?'

'If I tell you something, will you swear to keep it secret?'

'OK,' said Grace, intrigued.

'Swear.'

'I swear.'

'I saw my drill teacher, Mr Pawlek, taking pictures of the naval base. And I know this might sound really mad...but...well, I think he might be a German spy.'

'God!' This was far more exciting a secret than Grace had expected – it was like something from the Enid Blyton stories she read. 'What makes you think that?' she asked.

'There was something about the way he was doing it. It just didn't feel right. They've loads of posters in Liverpool warning you about spies, so I know the kind of stuff they do."

'Like what?'

'Checking out airfields, and ports, and beaches where landing craft could come ashore. And recording troop movements and where important factories are that could be bombed. All that stuff.'

'And you really think that's what he was at?'

'I don't *want* to believe it, because I like him.'

'But you're still suspicious?'

Barry nodded. 'There were a couple of other things too.'

'What?' asked Grace excitedly.

'Well, he always made it sound normal, but he's asked me a lot about my dad. Where his ship is, and all that. And he quizzed me about Mum too. She works in a factory making aeroplane parts – he was dead keen to know where the factory is.'

'Right.'

'And there was one other thing, though maybe it's nothing,' said Barry.

'What?' asked Grace, fascinated.

'I asked him what football team he followed. He said it was a local team I wouldn't know, but when I asked more he said he grew up in Danzig.'

'So?'

'Mr Pawlek is supposed to be Polish. I looked up Danzig, and it's a Free City that's surrounded by Poland all right. But it used to be in Germany. Polish people call it *Gdansk*, but the German name is *Danzig* – and that's what he called it.'

'God,' said Grace again, her pulses racing a little. 'Maybe he really is a spy.'

Barry made a face. 'Or maybe he's just a drill teacher who's interested in ships.'

'But what if he *is* a spy?' said Grace, part of her wanting the more adventurous explanation.

'Then I can't let him away with it. But if I say it to my grandma or anyone else they won't believe me.'

'Why don't we check him out? Then if we got proof we could go to the police.'

'Would you be on for that?' asked Barry.

'Of course! We're friends, aren't we? And he's the enemy if he's spying on your family for the Nazis!'

Barry looked at her approvingly, and Grace could see that he was pleased to have an ally.

'We won't say anything to anyone,' said Grace, 'but Mr Pawlek will be our mission. And if he's a spy we'll catch him out!' She held out her hand to Barry. 'Agreed?'

'Agreed!'

Strong sunlight shone through the church's stained-glass windows, colouring the altar with beautiful bands of red, green and blue light. The lingering smell of incense scented the air as the choir sang the final hymn of the Mass, and although Barry wasn't especially religious, this morning he felt uplifted. He was in good spirits to begin with, yesterday having been a rewarding day. He had been glad when Grace had called in to make things up, and in addition to their friendship being back on track he had also received an exciting letter from his mother. Apart from all the usual news from Liverpool, there had been two great developments. Firstly, he had been given permission to attend the sports camp, and secondly,

Mum had managed to bring her summer holidays forward, and would be visiting Dublin in July.

So things were definitely looking up, with the one exception of his suspicions about Mr Pawlek. And even that situation felt less like a worry and more like an adventure now that he had shared it with Grace, especially since she was eager to check out the drill teacher. The first step was likely to be taken in the next couple of minutes, Barry suspected, as he followed Grandma out of their pew in the church, having already spotted both Grace and Mr Pawlek in the congregation.

They all came out of the garrison chapel into the warm June sunshine, the Mass-goers mingling on the church steps and on the gravel driveway.

'Good morning, Mrs Malone,' said Mr Pawlek, as he approached them. 'Good morning, Barry.'

'Morning, sir,' answered Barry, feeling an illogical sense of guilt, even though Mr Pawlek couldn't possibly have known that Barry had discussed him with Grace.

'Mr Pawlek,' said Grandma. 'Beautiful morning, thank God.'

'Yes, beautiful. And a lovely Mass; the choir sang very well.'

'Didn't they?' said Grandma, and Barry could see that the teacher's comments had won the approval of his devout grandmother. *Was that a deliberate tactic, the kind of thing that a spy would automatically do to win people's trust?*

'And thank you for Thursday,' she added, 'Barry really enjoyed the trip to Cobh.'

'Good,' said Mr Pawlek, turning to look Barry in the eye. 'Interesting place, isn't it?'

He couldn't know he had been spotted taking pictures at the harbour, could he? Barry tried to keep his response casual. 'Yes,' he said, 'I'd a great day.'

'Glad to hear it.'

'And he got some more good news yesterday, didn't you, Barry?' said his grandmother.

'Eh, yes. My mum is coming to Dublin in a couple of weeks,' said Barry in explanation.

'Excellent,' replied Mr Pawlek. 'Though I thought the factories normally take their holidays in August?'

'Yes,' answered Grandma, 'But Ellen's factory is–'

'Letting some staff off in July,' cut in Barry, not wanting his grandma to reveal any further details about the aircraft factory. He suspected that the way he had cut Grandma off sounded slightly rude, so he continued now, as though he had done it from innocent excitement. 'It's great!' he enthused, 'they only let a small number of people take their holidays in July, and Mum's going to be one of them!'

'That's good news all right,' said Mr Pawlek.

Out of the corner of his eye Barry saw Grace's mother queuing for the Sunday newspaper, and he looked around to find Grace making straight for them.

'Hello, Mrs Malone, Barry,' she said.

Barry and his grandmother returned her greeting, then

Grandma turned to the drill teacher. 'This is Grace Ryan, a friend of Barry's. Grace, this is Mr Pawlek from Barry's school.'

'Hello, Mr Pawlek,' said Grace, 'I've heard all about you.'

The teacher raised an eyebrow. 'Really?'

'Yes. Barry told me about your summer camp. And the trip to Cobh – that sounded really interesting.'

Barry felt his pulses starting to race and he hoped that Grace wouldn't arouse Mr Pawlek's suspicions.

He watched carefully now as the teacher looked at Grace with interest. 'Yes, I think our trip was a success. And as for the summer camp, you'd be welcome to join us – it's for girls as well as boys.'

'Thanks,' said Grace. 'But I'd have to ask my ma about it.'

'Of course.'

'Grace is staying with her grandfather, her home was bombed in the North Strand,' explained Grandma.

'Oh. I'm sorry to hear that,' said Mr Pawlek.

He sounded completely convincing, Barry thought, though of course if he was a spy he would have had plenty of practice at lying.

'Yes, the German's bombed us, even though we're neutral,' replied Grace, with a hint of challenge.

Barry knew that Grace was doing this deliberately to see how Mr Pawlek would respond. He hoped that she hadn't gone too far, yet at the same time he was fascinated as he watched his teacher's expression.

'A dreadful event,' Mr Pawlek said sympathetically. 'And a clear violation of Ireland's neutrality.'

If he really *was* German, then he was a cool customer, Barry decided. He was nervous that Grace might push too far with more comments or questions, and it was a relief when Grandma tapped Mr Pawlek on the arm and pointed out Grace's mother in the queue for the papers. The two women had met through Grace's granddad, and had hit it off well.

'Let me introduce you to Mrs Ryan, Grace's mother,' said Grandma, obviously pleased to be the one doing the introductions.

'Please do,' answered Mr Pawlek, following Grandma as she made for the newspaper queue.

Barry dropped a few steps behind and turned to Grace. 'Don't overdo the questions!' he whispered. 'We don't want him on guard,'

'OK.'

'So, what do you think?' he asked. 'Am I mad?'

Grace shook her head. 'No. I'd say you're probably right.'

'You really think so?'

'Yeah. There's something about him. But like you said, we have to get proof.'

'I've been thinking about that.'

'And?'

Barry smiled. 'I have a plan...'

CHAPTER 13

Grace cycled hard, rising out of the saddle to increase her speed. It was important not to lose sight of their quarry, as she and Barry tailed Mr Pawlek through the Phoenix Park. The trees in the People's Gardens were bathed in warm, early evening sunshine but Grace barely noticed as she concentrated on keeping up with Barry.

A day had passed since she had been introduced to Mr Pawlek after Mass, and now they were following Barry's plan of tailing the drill teacher after working hours, to see who he might meet or what he might do.

Although Mr Pawlek lived in a house on the far side of Manor Street from Kinsella's cake shop, there was a rear entrance that backed onto Norseman Place, and Barry had said that Mr Pawlek regularly came out that gate in the evening on his bicycle.

Grace didn't have a bicycle of her own like Barry, but she had borrowed Uncle Freddie's bike, which he rarely used at night. She had been worried that Freddie might not lend it, but when she had asked him he had been engrossed in a newspaper report on the war – the Nazis had launched a huge invasion of the Soviet Union yesterday – and her distracted uncle had readily agreed. Ma had warned her sternly to be careful on Freddie's bicycle, but

Granddad had winked at her as she was leaving and had slipped her a penny.

She was looking forward to buying sweets with it for herself and Barry after their mission, but for now her mind was on keeping the right distance between them and Mr Pawlek. It was important not to get too near, in case he might spot them behind him, and they had been especially careful when waiting for Mr Pawlek to exit the rear gate of his garden. It was equally important, however, not to lose their quarry, and at times they had had to pedal hard to keep up with the very fit drill teacher.

They cycled across the main road of the Phoenix Park, past the big statue of Lord Gough on his horse. Despite the importance of the job in hand Grace still smiled to herself, as she often did when she saw the statue of Lord Gough. When she had been very small and her father was alive, her oldest brother, Sean, who now lived in Boston, had told her that the man riding the horse was their da. With the innocence of a toddler Grace had believed him, and for years the family had referred to it as Da's statue. The thought brought a wry smile to her lips, but tonight for some reason Grace felt a little sad too. If only Da were still alive he would be able to help Ma find a new house for them to live in, and they wouldn't be charity cases, dependent on the generosity of Granddad and Freddie. But nothing was going to bring Da back now, and with her two sisters married and her brothers living in Boston and Glasgow it was just herself and Ma, and they would have to fend for themselves.

'Speed up, Grace, he's pulling away!' called Barry from over his shoulder.

'OK!' she answered, aware that she had let her mind drift. She closed the gap with Barry, then saw Mr Pawlek in the distance as he descended the incline past the Wellington monument towards the base of the hill at the Magazine Fort.

Grace felt a little tired, having done a full day in school followed by a couple of hours in the cake shop, but she was excited too to be following a man who might be a spy, and she cycled hard, determined to keep up with Barry.

They saw that Mr Pawlek was heading towards the Corkscrew Road that wound around the southern boundary of the park. Grace knew this area from picnics with Ma, and she realised that a problem was looming. Barry had said that they mustn't wear anything eye-catching, and that by keeping well behind their prey they should remain unnoticed. The Corkscrew Road, however, twisted back around on itself, so that even if they kept their present distance behind Mr Pawlek, he would be cycling towards them on the opposite side of several narrow valleys.

'Barry!' she called. 'If he stays on this road we'll have to pull back.'

'Why?'

'It snakes back on itself and he'll see us.'

'If we pull back too far we'll lose him.'

'Then we'll follow him another time. We can't be spotted.'

Barry looked uncertain, then suddenly Mr Pawlek solved the

problem for them. In the distance Grace saw him swinging his leg over the saddle of his bike and cruising to a stop at a park bench on the stretch of road before the sharp bends.

'Hop off quick!' said Barry.

Grace braked at once, and they quickly dismounted.

'Down into the grass!' said Barry. They pulled over onto the grass verge and lowered the bicycles, then dropped down onto the high grass, the air about them alive with birdsong. Barry took a pair of children's binoculars from the carrier of his bicycle.

'Baggsy first go on the binoculars!' said Grace. Barry hesitated, and Grace put her hand out as though confident that he would hand them over. 'I baggsied them,' she said. 'And I'll give them back to you in a minute. Promise.'

'OK,' said Barry reluctantly as he passed them over. 'And I mean a minute.'

Grace remained lying low but poked the binoculars out through the stalks of sweet-smelling grass, with the lenses up to her eyes. The binoculars weren't very strong, and she had to focus them to get a good image, but they still allowed her to see Mr Pawlek quite clearly as he sat on the bench.

'What's he doing?' asked Barry.

'Nothing. He's just sitting there like he's taking in the view.'

'Any sign of him leaving stuff? Or collecting anything from under the seat?'

Grace felt excited and hoped that the drill teacher might leave or collect a parcel.

'Well?' prompted Barry impatiently.

'No, he's just sitting there with his hands on his lap.'

'Maybe he's waiting for someone.'

Grace moved the binoculars in an arc, sweeping the surrounding area. 'No sign of anyone coming near him,' she said.

'Here, give us a look,' said Barry.

Grace handed over the binoculars, taking care not to let them glint in the sun. She had seen a film in the Fairview Grand with Ma where the Apaches captured a cavalry scout who had given away his position by letting the sun reflect on the lens of his binoculars, and she was determined not to make the same mistake. Instead, she enjoyed the sensation of being hidden while they stalked Mr Pawlek.

Of course it could all be a mistake, and perhaps he really was just a Polish drill teacher. But if he *was* a spy they had to stop him. Barry said that even in a neutral country like Ireland a German spy could be gathering all sorts of information. According to Barry, the Nazis would be interested in weather reports for naval operations and bombing raids, and the location of ports, airfields, and power plants. Even gossip about morale and conditions in Britain – where countless Irish people had relatives – would be valuable to his superiors in Berlin.

'Anything happening?' she asked.

'No,' said Barry. 'But spy-catchers have to be patient. I read about it in a book.'

'Right.'

'So no matter how long it takes, we wait here till he makes his next move. OK?'

'Absolutely' answered Grace, then she settled down comfortably in her hiding place, listening to the song of the birds, but ready for whatever might happen.

* * *

'No more English, no more French,
No more sitting on a cold hard bench,
No more tables, no more chairs,
Throw the teachers down the stairs!'

It was the traditional last-day-of-school song, and Barry and his classmates sang it with gusto during break time in the noisy school yard. The smell from the soap factory hung in the air, but Barry was used to it by now. As they sang, Charlie Dawson danced about playfully, as though conducting a choir. Most of the boys laughed at Charlie's antics, but Shay McGrath responded angrily when Charlie bumped into him.

'Watch where you're going, Dawson!' he snapped, grabbing Charlie by the front of his shirt.

'Sorry, Shay, I was just–'

'Just what? Just being thick, weren't you?'

'No, I...'

'Watch what you're doin',' the bigger boy said, still holding

Charlie by his shirtfront and drawing him closer. 'Or I'll burst your face!'

'OK, OK,' replied Charlie nervously.

McGrath suddenly released Charlie's shirt, pushed him away and then walked off.

'What's wrong with him?' asked Barry

'He just wants someone to take it out on,' answered Charlie, ruefully rearranging his shirt.

'Take what out on?'

'Didn't you hear? His father was out of work for months, so he's leaving to work in Birmingham.'

Barry could hardly believe his ears. 'What! After all McGrath's rubbish about Ireland for the Irish, and England being the enemy!'

'I'd say he heard all that from his da. And now his da's going to England – so it makes him look a bit stupid.'

'A bit stupid?' said Barry. 'He's a complete hypocrite!'

'That's McGrath for you.'

'And then he takes it out on you.'

Charlie shrugged resignedly. 'I'll just keep out of his way.'

'No,' said Barry, 'he needs to be set straight.'

'I wouldn't go near him right now.'

'No, Charlie, now is the right time. Back in a minute,' said Barry, then he set off across the schoolyard to where he could see McGrath with his friends Nolan and Byrne, the two boys who had picked on Barry and helped to cover him in ashes. Neither boy had ever crossed him again after the intervention by Johnny

Keogh, and Barry wasn't afraid of them now as he approached McGrath.

'I want a word with you,' he said.

McGrath turned and looked at him sullenly. 'I don't want a word with you.'

'Really? You didn't mind having lots of words before. Words about England, and how I should go back there. How England is Ireland's enemy, and English people shouldn't be in Ireland; we should clear off. So, will you still hate the English when they're putting food on your table?'

McGrath wouldn't meet his gaze and said nothing.

'Funny how your father changed his tune when it suited him.'

'Leave my father out of it,' said McGrath, and for once his voice was lacking in aggression and sounded almost emotional.

Despite himself, Barry couldn't help but feel a tiny bit sorry for the other boy. Knowing what it was like to miss an absent father, he could imagine what McGrath was feeling. But then he thought of all the misery that McGrath had caused by his bullying. He reminded himself that McGrath's gang had almost cost Grace her job when they had taken the money from the cake shop, and how only moments ago McGrath had picked on his friend, Charlie.

'You know what's gas?' said Barry. 'Your father will probably get on fine. Because loads of English people like the Irish. And loads of Irish people get on fine with the English. It's only thicks like you who cause trouble. And talking of trouble, stay away from Charlie Dawson if you know what's good for you.'

Barry knew he was taking a chance here, and he was far from sure that Johnny Keogh's protection could be extended to his friend as well as himself. He issued the warning in a confident tone, however, hoping that McGrath wouldn't be willing to take a chance on crossing Keogh.

McGrath made no reply, and Barry decided to go for broke. 'You won't be warned again,' he said. 'So lay off Charlie.'

McGrath looked like he was trying to find an answer that might save face, but Barry turned on his heel and walked away, leaving the class bully looking frustrated. Barry was delighted to have gotten the better of McGrath for once, and he continued back across the yard, noticing that Mr Pawlek had joined the rest of the boys from his class.

'Ah, Barry,' said the drill teacher. 'I've just been giving the boys details of the sports camp,' he said, handing Barry a sheet of paper with dates and time written on it. 'The first trip is next Monday morning, swimming at Dollymount Strand.'

'Thanks, sir, I'm looking forward to it.'

'I'll bet you are,' answered Mr Pawlek, his pale blue eyes meeting Barry's.

Barry felt uncomfortable, but told himself it was his imagination. *The teacher surely couldn't know about his suspicions – could he?* No, Barry told himself, he and Grace had been really careful to stay out of his sight when they had followed him to the Phoenix Park on Monday evening.

That night had actually turned out to be a bit disappointing, in that Mr Pawlek hadn't met anyone, and didn't appear to have used the park bench as a drop-off point either to leave or pick up anything.

Still, there was something about the way Mr Pawlek looked at him now. It was almost as though he were weighing him up, and it put Barry on guard. The teacher was smart, and strong and fit. Barry still wasn't sure that he was a spy, but if he was one, he would be a formidable enemy.

I'm going to have to be careful, he told himself as he held Mr Pawlek's gaze and smiled casually back at him. *I'm going to have to be very careful.*

CHAPTER FOURTEEN

Grace nervously lowered her teacup and tried to get up the courage to ask Ma the question that had been on her mind all through dinner. Yesterday she had finished school for the summer, and when she had been working in the cake shop this afternoon Miss Kinsella had offered her extra working hours over the coming months. Miss Kinsella obviously meant well, but Grace didn't want the extra work. Instead, she had been planning to ask Ma if she could attend the sports camp with Barry for a couple of weeks.

The fact that Ma worked hard in the shirt factory made Grace feel guilty about asking for money for the summer camp. But she told herself again that it was just for two weeks. Besides, she could still work at weekends, and after that she could work as many hours as Miss Kinsella gave her. And although she couldn't say it to Ma, it was important to take the opportunity to get close to Mr Pawlek, if she and Barry were to find out if he really was a spy.

Grace pushed aside her cup, took a breath and then spoke up. 'Ma, I ... I wanted to ask you something.'

Her mother had been listening patiently as Uncle Freddie gave a mini lecture on the progress of the Nazis in their recent invasion of the Soviet Union. Now, though, she turned away from him and looked enquiringly at Grace. 'What is it, love?'

'I was wondering...I was hoping maybe I could go to the sports camp with Barry.'

Ma looked a little troubled. 'I don't know, Grace. How much would that cost?'

'It's three shillings a week. But I could pay some of that with the money I earn in the cake shop.'

'But you wouldn't *be* in the shop if you were at sports camp. And Granddad said Miss Kinsella is going to offer you extra hours.'

Granddad – who might have been a sympathetic ally – wasn't eating with them, having gone off to a card night. 'She offered me extra hours this afternoon,' said Grace, 'I was just going to tell you.'

'I hope you took them,' said Freddie.

Grace felt like telling him that this was between herself and Ma, but instead she responded to her mother. 'I thanked her for offering, and I told her I'd check with you first. You see I could still work on Saturdays, and when the camp is over I'd work all the hours she offers me. Please, Ma, can I?'

'Come on, now, Grace,' said Freddie firmly. 'You shouldn't put your mother on the spot like that.'

Grace suspected that he was taking this strict line to impress Ma, and she felt a surge of anger.

'You're not my father!' she said.

'Don't cheek your Uncle Freddie,' said Ma immediately.

'But he shouldn't be–'

'Don't argue with me, Grace,' said Ma, calmly but firmly. 'You're a guest here and you won't cheek your uncle under his own roof. Now, apologise, please.'

Grace could see that Freddie hadn't been expecting her to take him on, and she realised that even if she apologised he had still gotten the message loud and clear.

'Sorry,' she said politely, but with just enough reluctance to let him know that she was only saying it because she had to.

Freddie nodded stiffly in acknowledgement.

Grace looked at Ma and saw that her mother had taken no pleasure in chastising her. If anything she sensed that Ma was upset by denying her the two weeks of sports camp. And suddenly, despite wanting to help Barry solve the mystery with Mr Pawlek, Grace felt really bad. Ma worked long hours, she tried to keep everyone happy, and she watched every penny, saving for the day when she could afford to rent a place of their own.

'I'm sorry, Ma,' said Grace, this time sincerely. 'Look, I don't have to do the camp. I'll tell Miss Kinsella I'm taking the extra hours.'

Ma looked thoughtful. 'Maybe…maybe there's a compromise. Could you do some of the extra shifts, but go to the sports camp part-time?'

'Yeah, I'd say I could!' said Grace, her spirits rising. 'I can ask Mr Pawlek.'

'If you were doing it part-time then the fee would be less,' said Ma. 'And if you were still working extra hours that might cover it.'

'Miss Kinsella mightn't agree to that,' said Freddie.

'She's agreeable on most things, and I get on well with her,' said Grace, trying not to sound annoyed at Freddie for raising an objection.

'And she's a great friend of Granddad's', said Ma. 'I'd say she'll oblige you if Mr Pawlek will. So if you want to check it out with him, love?'

'Thanks, Ma, that's great!'

'When will you ask him?'

'Tonight!' said Grace, pleased at the turn of events, and thrilled to have an excuse for calling on a possible spy.

Barry had been wrestling with his conscience when Grace called for him. He had followed the newspaper reports of Hitler's invasion of the Soviet Union and part of him was pleased that millions of Russians would now be fighting against the Nazis. It meant that his father and the rest of the British forces would no longer be battling on alone. But he also knew that thousands of people would die because of the Nazi invasion, and he couldn't decide if it was right or wrong to be pleased.

Grace, however, didn't agonise over things, and when she called in and they discussed it, her answer had been simple. If the Russians played their part in fighting Hitler, then so much the better – and he shouldn't be such a worrier. Then she had told him her good news. Barry was delighted that Grace's mother was letting her go to sports camp, and he hoped that Mr Pawlek would agree to Grace attending part-time.

As they made their way through the hazy sunlight of the summer evening towards the teacher's house, Barry felt his pulses starting to race a little. The more contact he could generate with Mr Pawlek, the more chance there was of discovering if he really was a spy. It was tricky, though, because the last thing he wanted was to make Pawlek suspicious. He remembered the morning when they had all met after Mass, and how Grace had deliberately referred to the German bombing of the North Strand. She had done it to see how the teacher would react, but she would need to tread carefully today.

'When we get to his house, Grace, watch your step,' he said. 'OK?'

'How do you mean?'

'We want to suss him out. But don't push *too* hard with questions; we don't want him on guard.'

'I'll be careful. But he's not going to *tell* us he's a spy – we have to take some risks.'

'I know. But first we have to get close to him. All right?'

'OK.'

They turned the corner into Manor Street, then walked towards where Manor Street became Stoneybatter. Opposite the entrance to Stanhope Street convent, Grace's new school, was a terrace of houses with neat front gardens. The two friends opened the garden gate, then made their way to the front door of the teacher's house.

'It's a big enough place for him to be living in all by himself,' said Grace.

'Yeah, I suppose it is,' agreed Barry.

'Must cost a fair bit to rent. Are drill teachers paid that well?'

'I don't know.'

'If they're not, and he can still afford it, that's another reason he might be a spy – they'd be given money.'

It was a good point, Barry thought, but he raised his hand anxiously. 'Keep your voice down.'

'It's OK, the windows are all closed,' answered Grace as they ascended the steps leading to the hall door.

'Well,' said Barry. 'Ready?'

'Yeah.'

Barry lifted the knocker and knocked twice. He made himself breathe deeply, not wanting to appear anxious. He heard a sound in the distance, then footsteps approaching.

'Bingo!' said Grace with a grin.

In spite of his nervousness Barry smiled back at her, then he turned to the hall door as it swung open.

'Hello, Mr Pawlek,' said Barry, 'I hope we're not bothering you.'

The teacher looked surprised to see them, but he recovered quickly. 'Barry, Grace. What can I do for you?'

'I hope you might be able to do me a favour, Mr Pawlek,' said Grace. 'I'd love to join your sports camp.'

'Good. You'll be very welcome.'

'But the thing is, I have to work extra hours in the cake shop now that school is finished.'

'Ah.'

'So I was wondering if maybe I could come to the sports camp at the times when it doesn't clash with the shop?'

'Well, that's not how it's normally done…' said Mr Pawlek.

'I know, but I'd really love to be part of it,' said Grace.

Mr Pawlek looked at her, his pale blue eyes appraising, then Barry felt encouraged when the teacher smiled.

'Very well, if you're that eager, we'll fit you in.'

'That's great,' said Barry.

'Yeah, thanks very much, Mr Pawlek,' said Grace. 'And eh…my ma was wondering about the cost…'

'We'll make it *pro rata*.'

'What's that?' asked Grace.

'If you come half the time you pay half the price, if you come three-quarters, you pay three-quarters. Is that fair?'

'Yes, very fair. Thanks for fitting me in.'

'You're welcome.'

'I'm really looking forward to the sports, sir,' said Barry, hoping that if they got the teacher chatting he might invite them inside. To his disappointment, Mr Pawlek nodded pleasantly but in a manner that suggested he was finishing up.

'Yes, I'm sure we'll all enjoy it,' he said. 'Barry will give you the dates, Grace, he has the paperwork. I look forward to seeing you whenever you can make it. Good evening.'

'Good evening, sir,' said Barry.

'Good evening, Mr Pawlek, and thanks again,' said Grace.

The drill teacher nodded in farewell and shut the door, then Barry and Grace made for the gate.

'What do you think?' asked Barry.

'It's brilliant he let me join.'

'Yeah, he was nice about it.'

'Dead nice,' said Grace as they stepped out onto the street and started for home in the evening sunshine. 'But I still think you're right and that he's a spy.'

'Yeah?'

'He never asked us in. I bet he had stuff out he didn't want us to see.'

'Could be.'

'Any normal person would invite a visitor in,' said Grace.

'In Ireland they probably would – and in Liverpool,' said Barry. 'But maybe they've different customs in Poland.'

'Or *Germany*.'

'Maybe.

'And that thing *pro rata*. Were they German words'?

'No, that's Latin,' said Barry, 'I did it in school.'

'Oh.'

'You know, it's kind of weird, Grace. When I saw him in Cobh, I really felt there was something suspicious. But then he's dead nice, like he was now about the money.'

'He was decent all right. But acting really nice – wouldn't that be clever if you *were* a spy? You're sound, so everybody likes you and tells you things?'

'Yeah.'

Grace looked thoughtful. 'I've seen films with my ma about spies. And do you know what they always have?'

'What?'

'A radio transmitter. I bet he has one hidden in that house.'

'Gosh,' said Barry, excited by the idea. 'If we found that, we'd have our proof.'

'Maybe we could get in when he's not around?'

'Breaking in is a crime. We could be arrested.'

'Spying for the Nazis is a crime.'

It was true, Barry reflected. He remembered the night of the devastating air raid on his hometown and how he had sworn that some day he would find a way to fight back. *This was his chance.* Because if Mr Pawlek was a Nazi agent, he couldn't let him away with it.

'You're right,' he said. 'So whatever has to be done, let's do it.'

CHAPTER FIFTEEN

Grace screamed as she plunged down into the sea. The water was as warm as it ever got in early July, but squealing because of the temperature was part of the fun of swimming in the Irish Sea.

It was Grace's first day at the sports camp and already she knew that she was going to love it. Barry had introduced her to Charlie Dawson and some of Charlie's friends, and she had also met several girls that she knew from her new school in Stanhope Street. Everyone had been relaxed and friendly, and Mr Pawlek had led them on a cycle from Stoneybatter to Dollymount strand. They had found a nice spot in the sand dunes where they would later have a picnic lunch, and then Mr Pawlek had brought them down to the water for a swim.

She was really glad that Ma had allowed her to join part-time, despite Freddie having tried to show off by raising his objection. She knew that Ma was only being friendly to Freddie – like she was with everyone – but Freddie was too silly to see that and was still trying to impress her. Why couldn't he be like Granddad was with Miss Kinsella, just good friends?

But she wasn't going to worry about any of that right now. Firstly, because cycling and swimming in the sun was so much fun, and secondly, because she had a plan, and she was going to put it into action very soon. She swam towards where Barry was larking about with Charlie.

'Freezing, isn't it?' he said.

'It's not so bad once you get down,' said Grace, 'but I think I'm going to go in.'

'What's wrong?' said Barry.

Grace stood up and held her side. 'I'm after getting a cramp.'

'Better go in all right, Grace,' said Charlie. 'I heard a boy got a cramp at the Hole-in-the-Wall, and he was carried away in the current.'

'Thanks, Charlie!' said Grace.

'I'm only saying.'

'Do you want me to go back to the dunes with you?' asked Barry, playing his part.

'No, you stay here,' answered Grace with a wink, when Charlie wasn't looking.

'Should we tell Mr Pawlek?' asked Charlie.

'I'm sure Grace doesn't want a big fuss,' said Barry quickly.

'Definitely not,' agreed Grace, 'it's just a cramp. I'll see you later.'

Grace looked around and spotted Mr Pawlek throwing a water polo ball with some of the other boys. She moved off quickly while he was distracted. She waded in through the small waves that were lapping the beach. Without breaking stride she picked up her towel and wrapped it around herself, then made her way across the dried seaweed and on into the dunes. The sun was hot in a clear blue sky and once she left the beach behind the breeze dropped off and she felt warmer. She reached the small valley in the sand dunes where they had left their bags, and swiftly towelled herself dry.

She was shielded from view here, but her mouth had gone dry and her stomach was tight with tension. Ignoring her nerves, she crossed to Mr Pawlek's bag and unzipped it. She didn't know what she might find, but she and Barry had hatched this plan to check out the contents of the teacher's bag. If their hunch was right, the bag might contain something suspicious like coded lists of names, or drawings of military installations, or even a gun.

Grace sifted through the bag, taking care not to disturb its contents too much. She saw Mr Pawlek's dry clothes, wrapped sandwiches, barley sugar sweets, fruit and a soft drink. She continued rooting and found calamine lotion – presumably in case anyone got sunburned – and sticking plasters and a couple of bandages. There was no sign of a gun, but her hand did reach something solid over at the side of the bag. Grace gently pulled it out and saw that it was a small camera in a hard case. Her pulses raced a little faster as she realised that this might be useful. Supposing the pictures of the naval base in Cobh were on this roll of film? Or some other military site? That would certainly suggest that Mr Pawlek was up to no good.

If she took the camera and got the film developed they might have some hard evidence. But then again, if the film consisted of innocent photographs, she would have made herself a thief for nothing. And Mr Pawlek might suspect her, as the only person who had been alone in the dunes when his camera went missing. *Was it worth the risk of taking it?*

She hesitated, not sure what to do, then on impulse she put the camera back. Her fingers groped further into the bag and came to something soft that felt like leather. Grace withdrew it and saw that it was a wallet. Part of her felt guilty for snooping into someone else's private affairs, but if Mr Pawlek was an enemy agent she couldn't allow herself to be that prim and proper.

Her heart was pounding now, but she went ahead and opened the wallet. There were four Irish pound notes in it, and behind a clear window was a photograph of Mr Pawlek with a good-looking woman with blonde hair. *His German girlfriend?* There was also his ration book, a library card for Capel Street library, and assorted coins in a side pouch. There was a folded list of all the children attending the sports camp, their names written in small, neat handwriting. There were separate lists of boys and girls, and notes regarding which activities would take place each day. *An organised man, like you'd expect from a spy*. But there were no letters in German, no lists of contacts, no suspicious drawings.

Grace had a sudden thought and she slipped her fingers into the pouch of the wallet to remove the photograph, hoping that something might be written on the back. *Berlin 1938*, maybe, or *Love Always, Gretel*.

She felt her excitement mounting, then she had the photograph extracted and she turned it over. It was completely blank. Grace felt disappointed. She carefully replaced the picture and checked the remaining pockets of the wallet. She found several stamps and a brochure for a series of piano recitals of classical music. She put the wallet back in the bag, then felt around the base and sides of the kitbag, seeking any irregularity that might suggest a secret hiding place. She was still feeling her way along the side of the bag when she was startled by a call of 'Grace!'

It was Barry. Grace's heart thumped even more loudly, knowing that the cry from Barry was a warning. She immediately replaced Mr Pawlek's bag where she had picked it up and, keeping low, scurried across the sand dunes to where her own bag lay. She had just sat down when Mr Pawlek strode in between the dunes, followed by Barry. They were both wet from swimming but had towels wrapped around their shoulders.

'Grace,' said Mr Pawlek. 'I'm told you weren't well?'

Grace rose and tried to keep her voice normal, even though her heart was racing madly from the near miss and her face felt flushed. 'It was nothing much,' she said. 'Just a cramp, but I didn't think I should swim.'

'That was sensible,' said Mr Pawlek. 'Is your stomach upset?'

'Not really. I'll be fine.'

'Let me get you a barley sugar sweet,' suggested Mr Pawlek, and he crossed to where Grace had replaced his bag. He hesitated for a second, and Grace swallowed hard. *Had she put the bag back exactly where he had left it*? She wasn't certain and she felt tiny beads of perspiration forming on her forehead.

'If I get a cramp can I have one too, sir?' said Barry playfully.

Grace knew that Barry had picked up on her unease and that he was trying to distract the teacher.

Mr Pawlek opened his bag, taking out the barley sugar sweets. 'Why don't we all have one?' he said.

He smiled. Grace wasn't sure if it was just her guilty imagination but she felt that the smile didn't quite extend to his eyes. *Had he noticed something with the bag? She wasn't sure.*

The teacher handed out the sweets, his gaze fixed on Grace for a moment. Maybe he was only looking at her to be sure she was all right, she reassured herself.

'What game are we playing after lunch, sir?' asked Barry.

'Volleyball.'

'Great.'

Barry and Mr Pawlek chatted about the sports planned for later, and Grace sucked her barley sugar sweet, her pulses finally slowing down. On balance she felt that she had gotten away with searching the bag, but in checking out the drill teacher she would have to be careful in future. She glanced at his powerfully built physique, avoiding his alert blue eyes. One wrong move with this man, she thought nervously, could easily lead to disaster.

Grandma Peg blessed herself from the holy water font in the hall, then turned to Barry. 'I'm just going down to the Friary for the Third Order meeting. I'll see you later, love.'

'OK, Grandma.'

'Any special intention you want me to pray for?'

'Yeah. That we win the Sweepstake – and Hitler gets a really bad toothache!'

'You're an awful little pagan, so you are!' said Grandma, but she was laughing despite herself.

'Just as well I have you to pray for me then,' said Barry with a grin. His grandmother was more pious than his own parents, and for years she had been in a popular religious group called the Third Order that was devoted to St Francis, and that met in the Friary in Church Street.

'Seriously, is there anything you want me to pray for?'

'That Mum and Dad are safe,' answered Barry. 'And that Uncle George is OK in the prison camp.'

'They're all on my list already, but I'll pray for them again today.'

'Good,' said Barry.

'And don't worry, love. Saint Francis has never let me down yet.'

'No,' said Barry, wishing he was as confident about it as Grandma Peg. He prayed every day for his parents' safety, and he knew that Grandma said a decade of the rosary in her bedroom every night for Dad, her only son. But although Barry was comforted by the thought of all the prayers offered for Dad, it had struck him that there must be good people in Germany too. And if they were religious and prayed for their sons, what happened then? If Dad's ship was fighting a German U-boat, who was God supposed to protect? It wasn't a question he felt he could ask Grandma, but it gnawed at him a little all the same.

The other thing he couldn't tell Grandma about was his worry regarding Mr Pawlek. Grandma thought the drill teacher was 'an absolute gentleman', her greatest compliment, and she would dismiss his suspicions as youthful nonsense.

It was a pity that Grace had found nothing incriminating in Mr Pawlek's kitbag a couple of days previously in the sand dunes. But the fact that all of the bag's contents looked innocent proved nothing – except that Mr Pawlek was careful if he *was* a spy.

'Ah, here's the post,' said Grandma as the letter box snapped open and shut and a couple of envelopes fell down into the hall. Grandma moved to retrieve them. 'One from Cork, that will be Bernie,' she said.

Barry looked hopefully at the other envelope as Grandma slipped the letter from her sister into her bag.

'I'll save that for later,' she said. 'And this is for you, Barry. English stamp and your mother's handwriting.'

'Great!' said Barry taking the letter from her. He waved goodbye to his grandmother as she went out the door, then made for the kitchen and sat down at the table to savour the letter.

He was really looking forward to seeing Mum again and he opened the envelope, hoping to hear if she could take her holidays in early July. To his delight, the news was good, and Mum said that she was hopeful of being in Dublin sooner rather than later. She filled him in as usual on all the local news, and made him laugh with her colourful description of a day trip to Hilbre Island,

and of how she and her friend Janet from work had nearly been caught out by the tide. She passed on greetings from his friends on the road, and to Barry's relief confirmed that the *Luftwaffe* raids on Liverpool had stopped for the moment. Best of all, she had received a letter from Dad, who was well, and who was learning to play the ukulele – on which he promised to play George Formby's hit 'Leaning on a Lamppost' when he next got home!

Barry felt a funny mixture of happiness at being drawn again into the world of his parents, yet sadness that all three of them were so far apart. Still, Mum would be here soon, he told himself, and if Mr Pawlek *was* actually spying for the Nazis then Mum would soon sort him out.

First, though, he had to get some solid evidence. Mum loved him and backed him in most things, but she also claimed he had a vivid imagination. He could well imagine her laughing off his story that a foreign teacher was a German spy. So hard proof was what he needed. And even though it was risky, tomorrow night he was going to try to get it. He put down the letter, his thoughts racing as he rehearsed in his mind how he hoped to do it.

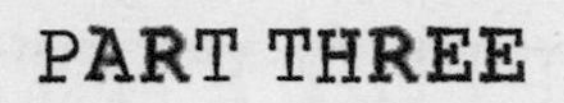

PART THREE

PROOF

CHAPTER FIFTEEN

Grace sprinted excitedly up Manor Place. She rounded the corner into Norseman Place where she saw Barry pretending to be engrossed with hopping a ball on a hurley. In fact he was discreetly keeping watch on the rear entrance to Mr Pawlek's house, just as Grace had been watching the front entrance on Manor Street.

Barry looked up expectantly. 'Well?'

'He went out. He's dressed up, so I'd say he's gone somewhere.'

'Right,' said Barry.

'Now's our chance,' said Grace, feeling really nervous, but excited at the same time. It was three days since she had searched the teacher's bag in the sand dunes, and after a lot of discussion she and Barry had decided that Saturday night – when most adults went out – would be their best opportunity to enter Mr Pawlek's house.

Grace looked up and down the road. Norseman Place consisted of a terrace of cottages, opposite which were the back garden walls of houses in Manor Street, including the house rented by Mr Pawlek. Grace had already checked the rear entrance door, but it was locked. She was going to have to climb over the wall, which, fortunately, wasn't too high. She could see small children playing at the far end of the road, and a middle-aged woman was walking along the pavement towards herself and Barry.

'Give us a go with the hurley, will you?' said Grace.

Barry handed over the hurley and Grace began tapping the ball up in the air. The woman walked past, paying little heed to the two friends. Grace waited until the woman had rounded the corner, then she looked up and down the road again. Apart from the small children it was all clear. Of course, someone could be looking out the front window of one of the cottages, so Grace began to hit the ball higher in the air, then contrived to knock it over the wall into Mr Pawlek's back garden

'Blast!' she said in mock annoyance. 'Give us a hoosh up, Barry!'

Barry stood with his back to the garden wall and held his hands together, fingers intertwined. Grace ran towards him and placed her foot in the locked hands. Barry swiftly lifted her up in the air, and she gripped the top of the wall. She hoisted herself up to sit on it, then swung round, lowered herself by her arms and dropped down into the garden. She felt a jolt go up through the soles of her feet, then heard the sound of Barry's voice from the far side of the wall.

'I'll help find the ball!' he cried.

Grace heard the sound of running footsteps as Barry ran at the wall, then he too hoisted himself up and sat on the top, before swinging over and dropping down into the garden. He immediately pocketed the ball, and they both moved swiftly to the back door of the house.

'Worth a try,' said Grace softly as she reached out for the handle of the back door.

'Pity,' said Barry when the locked door didn't budge.

'OK, give us the knife,' she said.

Barry reached into his pocket and removed a flat table knife that he had wrapped in a handkerchief. Grace took it from him and approached a downstairs window, praying her plan would work. To her relief, the lock on the window was the same as the one she had noted on the front window of the house. Grace started to slide the flat blade of the knife between the upper and lower halves of the window. She had seen Ma doing this once when they were accidentally locked out, and the trick was to slide the knife in and then use it to push the lock sideways so the lower half of the window could be pulled up.

Grace got the knife in place and pushed, but nothing happened. She pushed again, but still the lock was too stiff.

'Here, let me try,' said Barry

But Grace felt that this was her suggestion, and she didn't want to be shown up by a boy, even her friend Barry. 'Hold on,' she said. She tried again, pressing with all of her strength, and suddenly the lock snapped sideways.

'Yes!' she whispered triumphantly, and Barry smiled and gave her a thumbs-up sign.

Without wasting any time, Grace slid the window up and climbed into what she realised was the kitchen. Barry followed immediately after her, quietly closing the window behind him. The kitchen was warm, and the dust they had disturbed on the window ledge danced in the beams of evening sunlight that filled the air.

'OK, let's split up like we said,' suggested Grace.

'All right,' answered Barry, making for the hallway so that he could climb the stairs and search the upstairs rooms, while Grace did the ground floor. 'Good hunting,' he said, with a nervous grin.

'You too,' replied Grace, trying for a grin in return, but feeling really frightened at what they were doing. Even though it looked like Mr Pawlek had gone out for the evening, she couldn't be sure he wouldn't return. The quicker they got this done the better, but at the same time there was no point breaking in if they were going to be too scared to search the place properly. Forcing her fears to the back of her mind, Grace began systematically searching the kitchen. She opened and examined drawers and presses, making sure to replace everything exactly as she had found it.

The most important thing that an enemy agent would have was a radio set for sending out signals in code, but Grace was also on the lookout for drawings, photographs or perhaps even a gun.

She searched the kitchen thoroughly, but found nothing suspicious. A little disappointed, Grace moved on to the pantry behind the kitchen and continued her search there. She reckoned that Barry was just as nervous as she was, but she was confident that he wouldn't lose his nerve, and would carefully check out the upstairs rooms, going through wardrobes and chests of drawers, and looking under the beds.

Grace worked her way through every press, cupboard and drawer in the pantry but found nothing out of the ordinary. She finally gave up on the pantry and kitchen, and was making for the downstairs living room and parlour when she met Barry coming down the staircase.

'Finished upstairs?' she said.

'Yeah, found nothing.'

'Is there an attic?'

'Yes,' said Barry, 'but it's high up. You'd need a ladder to reach it. He wouldn't want to get a ladder every time he sends a radio message.'

'No.'

'Why don't I do the front room here and you do the back one?' Barry suggested.

Grace nodded in agreement. 'OK.'

She moved into the living room. Like everywhere else in the house, Mr Pawlek had it neat and tidy, but it had a lived-in feel, with sheet music propped up on an opened piano and a newspaper on the table. *This is the place where he actually lives*, thought Grace. She felt a tingle of excitement run up her spine, as she sensed that they were closer to their quarry here than anywhere else in the house.

She worked her way around the room, noting that the piano piece was 'Für Elise' by Beethoven. *German music,* she thought, even though she knew that Beethoven was popular because he was a great composer, and not because he was German. *Still though…*

She worked her way methodically towards a curtained alcove on the far side of the room, then stopped. On a small coffee table a map of Europe was spread out. The recent Nazi advances during the invasion of the Soviet Union were marked on the map, and Grace felt another little shiver up her spine.

'Barry!' she called, 'look at this.'

Barry came in from the other room, and Grace pointed out the map to him.

'So he's interested in the war in Russia,' he said thoughtfully.

'I know it's not exactly proof,' said Grace.

'No, loads of people follow the war. I do, your Uncle Freddie does...'

'Even so, it's the first thing we've seen that could be suspicious. Nothing in the front room?'

'No, I was just about to come and join you. What's behind the curtain?' said Barry, indicating the curtained alcove.

'I don't know,' said Grace, 'I was working my way towards it.'

They both moved across the room, and Grace pulled back the curtain. The alcove wasn't very deep, and neatly stowed against the wall were a folded ironing board, a sweeping brush and a mop and bucket. Of more interest, however, was a press set into the wall. It had a door that was designed to swing outwards. Grace stared at it, her pulses quickening. *The door was sealed with a new-looking padlock.*

Grace looked at Barry and could see that he grasped the significance at once.

'What would a drill teacher have that needs to be locked away behind a curtain?' he said.

'Exactly.' Grace started to examine the lock when suddenly she was startled by a series of loud knocks on the heavy wooden front door.

'Mother of God!' she said, her heart seeming to explode in her chest.

Barry looked scared too but he whispered, 'It can't be Mr Pawlek, he wouldn't knock.'

'Maybe it's someone who saw us coming in over the back wall. Maybe it's the police!'

'Oh no!' said Barry. 'Will we run out the back?'

'Let's see who it is first,' said Grace, forcing herself to think straight despite her thumping heart. 'I'll run upstairs and peek out the window!'

Before Barry could respond, Grace ran from the kitchen. Moving lightly so that her footsteps wouldn't be heard, she ascended the stairs two steps at a time. She quickly made her way to the window of what was a spare bedroom, then very cautiously pulled back a portion of the lace curtain. She prayed with all her might not to see a policeman on the doorstep. When she looked down she saw a well built man standing slightly back from the door.

A detective? Grace felt a surge of panic. *What would happen if he caught them? And how on earth could they possibly explain what they were doing breaking into the teacher's house?* And then Grace felt a wave of joyous relief when she saw what the man had in his hands. He was a ticket seller, calling to try and sell raffle tickets for some charity.

Grace breathed out deeply and stepped back from the window as the man turned away. It had been a terrifying moment, and she decided now that they had learnt all that they could for tonight. *Time to get out of here*, she thought, then she re-crossed the room, made for the stairs and descended at speed.

CHAPTER SIXTEEN

'When the Saints go Marching In' played on the gramophone, and Barry tapped in time with his foot as he relaxed on Sunday night in the parlour of Grandma's house.

'Great song, Grace. Full marks to Uncle Freddie for once,' he said with a grin, indicating the gramophone record that his friend had borrowed from her uncle's collection.

'He's still an eejit. You should have heard him in the park today, trying to butter Ma up.'

'What did he say?' asked Barry.

Grace wickedly mimicked her uncle trying to sound solicitous: 'Could I interest you in a ripple ice cream, Nancy?'

Barry laughed, and Grace smiled ruefully.

'Easy for you to laugh. But I was praying for Ma to give him the brush off. He'd make you sick when he's like that.'

Barry hesitated, but then felt that as a friend he should alert Grace. 'Look, I know, Grace, you don't want to hear this, but maybe...maybe your mum likes him, you know?'

'Do you mean *fancies* him?'

'Well, yeah.'

'She doesn't.'

'How do you know?'

'Because I asked her.'

Barry was taken aback. 'Really? You asked your mother that?'

Grace nodded. 'It was awful. I didn't know where to start. But it was driving me mad, and I was really worried that maybe, just maybe, she did like him. So in the end I blurted it out.'

'What did she say?'

'That Freddie and Granddad had been really good to us, so we had to be nice, too. But she had no plans to re-marry. And if she ever had, Freddie would be the last man in the world she'd pick.'

'That's your problem solved then.'

'Not really. I mean *I* know now, and that's good. But she hasn't told Freddie. And he's the one who needs to know.'

'He'll probably catch on in the end.'

'The sooner the better. So, what did you do today?'

'I was in the park as well. Myself and Charlie took Blackie up to the dog pond for a swim.'

'Great.'

'Yeah, it was good fun. I needed something relaxing. I couldn't sleep for ages last night after we got back from Mr Pawlek's.'

'Me neither,' said Grace 'And when I *did* sleep I dreamt that your man knocking on the door really was the police. It turned into a sort of nightmare.'

Barry felt bad. 'Maybe I...maybe I shouldn't have dragged you into all this, Grace–' he began.

'Don't be daft!' said Grace, cutting him short. 'We're in this together. And yeah, it was scary last night, but I still wouldn't have missed it.'

'Sure?'

'Just try keeping me out of it!'

Barry felt a surge of affection and he smiled at Grace. 'Fair enough. So,' he added, 'have you thought about what we do next?'

Grace nodded. 'We know how to get into his house. Somehow we have to get into the locked press.'

'Yeah.'

Just then the record came to the end.

'Here, put on "Jeepers Creepers" again,' said Grace, 'I really like that one.'

'OK.' Barry was reaching out to take the record from its sleeve when he heard a knock on the front door. Grandma was at Sunday evening Benediction in the church, and he wasn't expecting any callers.

He thought nervously about their break-in the previous evening. They had re-locked the window and had exited the house through the front door, as though they were visitors leaving, and he had collected the hurley before heading home. But of course they could still have been spotted and reported to the police. Supposing this was the police, calling to question him?

'Are you not going to get that?' asked Grace.

'Let's just see who it is,' said Barry as he crossed to the window. He looked out carefully. There was no sign of a police car parked outside, but he couldn't see who was standing at the front door.

'Well?' said Grace.

'I can't see. If it's the police, say we climbed over for the ball last night, but admit nothing else, OK?'

'OK,' answered Grace uneasily.

'Right,' said Barry then he took a deep breath and made for the hall.

There was another series of knocks, and Barry called out 'Coming.' He reached the door, gathered himself for a moment, then opened it.

'Surprised?' said the caller.

Barry stood unmoving, rooted to the spot in shock.

'Looks like you are.'

Barry's face suddenly lit up with a huge smile. 'Mum!' he cried and the next thing he knew he was embraced in the arms of his teary-eyed mother.

* * *

Granddad hummed along happily as Joe Loss played on the radio.

'Ah, your favourite, Granddad,' said Grace as she came into the kitchen and recognised the bandleader's version of 'In the Mood'. She had arranged to go round to Viking Place this evening for a game of hopscotch with May Bennett, but she paused now on finding Granddad alone.

'Wonderful musician,' said Granddad, 'great rhythms.'

'Yeah, I love the way you want to move to the music. And of course there's one other great thing about him,' she said playfully.

'What's that?'

'He's not Mantovani!' said Grace, and Granddad laughed at the fact that she had picked up on the Joe Loss versus Mantovani arguments that he had with Freddie.

'That Mantovani fella – he's too lush to be wholesome!' said Grace, mimicking her grandfather.

He laughed goodnaturedly. 'I wouldn't take that cheek from anyone but my favourite lodger.'

This was a running gag with Granddad. 'Sure I wouldn't say it to anyone but my favourite granddad!' Grace responded. This was a gag too, as Ma's father, her other grandfather, had died before she was born.

Granddad smiled. 'Well, while we're praising each other, you might as well know. Nellie Kinsella is very taken with you.'

'Really?'

'Yeah, she likes having you in the shop. Says you're a great little worker.'

Grace had been getting on well with Miss Kinsella, but it was still good to hear the compliment. 'That's nice of her.'

'No more than the truth. And Nellie's a good judge of character, mind.'

'Thanks. And...eh, how did you come to be friends with her?' asked Grace curiously.

'Sure myself and Nellie go back donkey's years.'

Grace raised an eyebrow. 'Oh?'

'Not like that, you scamp. When I was a carpenter in the distillery I worked with Nellie's brother, Jack, before he moved to Sheffield. And your granny, God be good to her, got to know Nellie, and we all played cards together.'

'Right,' answered Grace. The mention of carpentry had given her an idea, and she tried to make her next enquiry sound casual. 'Talking about being a carpenter, Granddad, can I ask you something about locks?'

'What about them?'

'Well, aren't carpenters involved when locks are put on doors?'

'Yes. I mean, locksmiths make the locks and keys, but carpenters often fit them. Why do you ask?'

'It's eh…it's this book I'm reading. The boy in it picks a padlock, and I was wondering how you do that?' Grace didn't like lying, but she couldn't tell Granddad the real reason behind her question.

He looked at her. 'You're not thinking of breaking in somewhere, are you?'

'No.'

'I don't want to hear from Nellie Kinsella that the jam for the jam slices has vanished!'

Grace was relieved that he was only joking. 'No, it's just that in this book the boy picks a lock to escape. But what do you actually *do*?'

'You have to put something into the lock that's manoeuvrable, but still stiff. Say, like a small nail file or a safety pin. Then you move it around, this way and that. What you're trying to do is trip the internal levers, the way a key would, so it springs open.'

'And is it hard to do? Like, would it take long?'

'It depends on the lock. And how lucky you are, and how patient.'

'Right.'

'What's the book about?'

Grace had to think quickly. 'It's eh, it's a kind of adventure story about a group of children who track down a gang of smugglers.'

'I see. Well, probably quicker to pick a lock in a book than in real life,' said Granddad.

'I suppose so,' said Grace. 'Anyway I better go, I'm meeting May.'

'Mind the trams!' said Granddad with a smile.

Grace smiled back, then made for the door, her mind playing over the words her grandfather had said. *It depends on the lock. And how lucky you are, and how patient*. There was only one way to find out. And that would mean going back to Mr Pawlek's house.

CHAPTER EIGHTEEN

Barry took aim, then shot the man twice in quick succession. They were standing on the busy pavement on O'Connell Bridge, and Barry's victim clutched his chest, then staggered backwards. Before Barry could open fire again he was shot himself by a cheery, middle-aged woman, and he doubled up in apparent pain from the imaginary bullet. Mum burst out laughing, and Barry joined in, thinking how lucky they were to have stumbled upon a 'shoot-up' with one of Dublin's best-loved street characters, the famous 'Bang Bang'.

Bang Bang was a simple-minded man in his thirties who carried a large metal key with which he 'shot' his fellow citizens, at the same time calling out his trademark cry of 'bang-bang'. The people of the city had taken to him, and they responded to his imaginary gunplay by returning fire or pretending to be shot. Whole streets of laughing people were sometimes left playing Cowboys and Indians in his wake, with Bang Bang starting the shoot-up before jumping on a passing bus or tram to make his escape.

Barry felt really happy now, this encounter with Bang Bang being the cap on a couple of great days. It had been a brilliant surprise when Mum had arrived two nights previously. She had treated Barry and Grace to ice cream that first night, and Barry was pleased when Mum and Grace got on well. Then Grandma Peg arrived back from Benediction and there had been a big fuss, after which Mum had moved her luggage into the spare room.

They stayed up late, planning what they would do during her two weeks of holidays. Mum understood that Barry loved the sports club, and she had agreed that he could continue attending events with Mr Pawlek and his friends, after which she would meet him so that they could have treats together. Trips to the zoo and the cinema were planned, but simply having Mum around was the best treat of all.

The one tricky moment was earlier today when he had to introduce Mum to Mr Pawlek. The sports club members had gone to the Phoenix Park for rounders and relay-races. Grace was working in the cake shop, so when the day's events ended there was a moment when Barry found himself with just Mum and Mr Pawlek. There was no choice then but to introduce them, something which made him nervous.

He couldn't show his mother any solid evidence against his teacher, but he was still afraid the man was an enemy agent, and that he might persuade Mum to let something slip about the war work she was doing in the factory. And if Mum revealed where the factory was located – which could easily happen during conversation – that information could find its way to Germany, and result in another *Luftwaffe* air raid.

'Mr Pawlek, this is my mother,' he had said, striving not to let his concern show. 'Mum, this is Mr Pawlek.'

The teacher smiled and gave a little bow before shaking hands. '*Madame*,' he said.

'Mr Pawlek,' said Barry's mother, smiling back. 'Nice to put a face to the name.'

'Likewise. Barry has told me all about you.'

'Really?'

'Yes, indeed. I trust your husband is safe and well?'

'He's fine, thank you.'

'Barry also told me about your own work, riveting aircraft. Very impressive!' said Mr Pawlek with a charming smile.

Mum smiled also and spoke to Barry in a lightly chiding tone. 'Now, Barry, you know what they say, "loose lips sink ships!" '

If only you knew, thought Barry. He tried for a rueful grin and said, 'I didn't give away anything too vital, Mum.'

Everyone laughed, but Barry felt on edge as his mother chatted to the drill teacher. To Barry's relief Mr Pawlek didn't press Mum about Dad's location, or ask where in Liverpool her factory was situated. Instead they chatted easily about Barry's progress in school – *popular and well-behaved!* – and life in Dublin. Barry discovered that Mr Pawlek found the rationing tiresome but enjoyed the varied musical entertainment that the city offered. When it emerged that both Mum and Mr Pawlek liked classical piano music, Mum told him of the concert pianists that she had seen performing in Liverpool. Barry was glad when the pleasantries finally ended without Mum revealing anything an agent might find useful.

After that he had taken the bus to town with his mother, and they had tea in Bewley's restaurant. Part of Barry had wanted to come clean and tell Mum about his suspicions, but he didn't want to spoil what had been a great day by making an accusation that his mother would very likely dismiss. And now as they prepared to head home after the Bang Bang incident, his caution was confirmed.

'You've a vivid imagination, Barry,' said Mum, laughingly referring to how convincingly he had entered into the shooting and being shot. 'But then you always had!'

'Really?'

'Must come with your Irish blood!'

Barry smiled, knowing his mother wasn't being entirely serious. But she clearly did believe that he had a strong imagination. *No, there was no point telling her a spy story that sounded half-baked.*

'Fancy an ice cream cone to finish the day off?' asked Mum

Barry couldn't think of any better way to finish the day, and he decided to put Mr Pawlek out of his mind for the rest of the evening. 'Do I fancy an ice cream cone?' he said, as though giving it serious consideration. 'Well, you know what Dad always says?'

'What's that?'

'Is the Pope a Catholic?'

Mum laughed. 'That's a yes, then.'

'That's a yes!'

'You're not going to believe this,' said Charlie Dawson, flopping down onto the grass beside Grace and Barry.

'Try me!' retorted Grace.

The sports club members were sitting on the bank of the River Liffey at the weir called the Salmon Leap, and the summer air carried the reedy smell of the river. Led by Mr Pawlek, they had cycled from the city through the Phoenix Park, then down the steep incline of Knockmaroon Hill into the scenic area of the Liffey Valley known as the Strawberry Beds.

'Whacker Wallace just told me the latest on Shay McGrath,' said Charlie, savouring his news.

Grace thought that Whacker was the silliest member of the sports club, but she was still interested in anything to do with Barry's former tormentor. Barry was interested too and he responded first.

'What about McGrath?'

'Well, you know the way his da is working in Birmingham now?'

'Yeah, he hates the English but takes their money,' said Barry.

'Maybe he doesn't hate them so much any more. Because he's moving the whole family over to Birmingham.'

'Really?' said Grace in surprise. But then again, maybe it wasn't that surprising. McGrath's father had been penniless and unemployed for months. He might well want to settle with his family in a place with plenty of war-time work.

'Means we won't have to put up with McGrath when school starts again,' said Charlie happily.

'Great,' said Grace. Now she wouldn't have to pay off Johnny Keogh with rhubarb tarts if Barry stayed on in Ireland. Not that she minded, really. Barry was a good friend, and she hoped that his mother would decide to keep him in Dublin for safety's sake. Grace didn't want the people in Liverpool to be bombed any further; she knew at firsthand how awful that was, but she still hoped Mrs Malone would leave Barry in his Grandma Peg's for fear of more raids.

She looked at Barry now, expecting him to be annoyed by the double standards of the McGrath family, but instead he was grinning.

'After all McGrath's rubbish about hating the English, he's probably going to end up with a Brummy accent!' said Barry. 'I love it!'

'It's eh...what do you call that thing about justice and a poem?' said Charlie.

'Poetic justice,' said Grace

'That's it, it's poetic justice,' said Charlie.

'Poetic justice? Tell me more,' said Mr Pawlek, approaching.

Grace hadn't heard the teacher coming up behind them. His tone was light-hearted and he looked with curiosity at Charlie.

'It's Shay McGrath, sir. He was always going on about England and the English. Now his whole family are moving there.'

'Are they?' said Mr Pawlek.

'Yeah, all nine of them,' said Charlie.

'Hard to know which would be worse,' said Barry, 'being invaded by Hitler or being invaded by the McGraths!'

Everybody laughed, but Grace felt that just like the day in the sand dune, Mr Pawlek's laugh didn't quite extend to his eyes. Seeing as the topic of invasion had been raised, she decided to be bold.

'Talking of invading, sir' she said, 'what's happening in Russia? Are the Germans still advancing?' Grace kept her tone innocent, but looked enquiringly at Mr Pawlek.

He shrugged easily. 'I don't know, Grace. I don't follow it all that closely.'

Liar! she thought to herself. *You've a map in your kitchen marking the front lines!*

Grace caught Barry's eye briefly and saw that he too recognised the significance of the teacher's answer. Any doubts that Grace might have had were gone now; an innocent man would have had no reason to lie.

'Anyway, enjoy your lunches,' said Mr Pawlek, smoothly moving on from the topic of the war. 'You can sunbathe for a while if you like, we won't be starting back till two o'clock.'

'OK, sir,' answered Charlie, then the teacher moved on to another group.

'That's some surprise about McGrath, isn't it?' said Charlie.

'Yes,' said Grace, exchanging a conspiratorial glance with Barry, 'you really never know what people are up to, do you?'

CHAPTER NINETEEN

'It's the end of an era,' said Grandma, as she left Sunday morning Mass at the garrison church and stepped out into the sunlight with Barry and Mum. The death had been announced during the Mass of the church's long-standing organist.

'I always hate to hear of a musician dying,' said Mum, who was a keen pianist herself, although more given to jazz and the classics than religious music.

'It's really sad,' said Grandma, 'he was only fifty-six.'

'That's not *that* young,' said Barry.

'When you're my age, fifty-six is young,' said Grandma with a wry smile.

Many of the congregation had been genuinely saddened, and everyone had prayed for the soul of the organist during the Mass. Now, though, Barry's spirits picked up on seeing Grace and her family chatting in the church grounds.

They approached the Ryans, and greetings were exchanged.

'Looks like you brought the good weather with you, Ellen!' said Freddie.

This was said in what Barry's dad would have called a 'hail-fellow-well-met' voice, and Barry wished that Grace's Uncle Freddie wouldn't always try to convince people that he was the life and soul of the party.

'Well, if we hadn't good weather in July, when would we have it?' said Mum easily.

'Very astute, Ellen, very astute. We're not dealing with muck here!' said Freddie.

Mum smiled, even though Freddie wasn't very funny, and Grace caught Barry's glance and raised her eyes to heaven. Barry winked back at her, then found himself going on alert as he saw Mr Pawlek approaching, the Sunday newspaper under the teacher's arm.

'Ah, Mr Pawlek' said Grandma.

'Mrs Malone – by two!' replied the drill teacher.

Barry watched as his mother smilingly returned the greeting, then Pawlek turned to him and Grace.

'Barry, Grace, how are you?'

'Fine, thank you,' answered Grace politely, though Barry picked up on a tiny hint of coolness.

'Fine, thanks, sir,' answered Barry a little more enthusiastically, not wanting to alert Pawlek to their reservations about him.

'Mr Pawlek, have you met the rest of Grace's family?' asked Grandma.

'No, I haven't had the pleasure.'

'You know Mrs Ryan. And this is Tom Ryan, and Freddie Ryan, Grace's grandfather and uncle.'

Mr Pawlek shook hands warmly with all of the group, and Barry noticed how good he was at being friendly and relaxed with people he had just met.

'I have to say, Mrs Ryan, your daughter is a great addition to our sports camp.'

'Thank you, Mr Pawlek,' said Grace's mother with a smile.

'And an excellent swimmer. Perhaps you taught her yourself – I could see you as an athlete?'

'Thanks for the compliment,' said Grace's mother, obviously pleased. 'But it was my late husband who taught Grace when she was small.'

'He did a fine job. Do you swim yourself?'

'No, I'm afraid not.'

'Maybe you should learn. I'm sure you wouldn't be long picking it up.'

'Nancy has a full-time job,' said Freddie. 'We don't all have teachers' hours and time for swimming.'

Freddie tried to make it sound light, but it was clear to Barry that he resented Mr Pawlek. Barry remembered what Grace had said about Freddie having a soft spot for her mother, and he was amused by Freddie's jealousy, though he made sure not to show it.

'I suppose, Mr Pawlek, you find the Irish summers cool enough?' said Mr Ryan, Grace's granddad, in a diplomatic move to change the subject. 'Compared to Poland, like?'

'Yes, we have warmer summers in Poland.'

Or in Germany, thought Barry. He caught Grace's eye and suspected that she was thinking the same thing.

'But then we have colder winters in Poland, so it balances out.'

'Sure isn't that the way with most things in life?' said Mr Ryan agreeably.

'Indeed it is,' said Grandma, 'I always say, God never closes one door but he opens another.'

The conversation descended into general chit chat, mostly about the weather, but Barry's ears pricked up when Mr Pawlek turned back to his mother and spoke to her.

'I'm glad I bumped into you, Mrs Malone,' he said, 'there was something I wanted to ask you?'

'Yes?'

Barry felt himself getting anxious, even though Pawlek's demeanour was relaxed.

'I don't wish to trespass too much on your holiday time, but there's an excellent piano recital in town tomorrow night. I wondered if you might like to attend as my guest?'

No! thought Barry, *find some reason to stay away from him!*

'Well…' said Mum and Barry could see that she was uncertain how to respond.

'It's Grieg's Piano *Concerto Number One*, Beethoven's *Moonlight Sonata*, some Chopin nocturnes, and Gershwin's *Rhapsody in Blue*, just so we don't get too stuffy!'

Barry could see that Mum was tempted, but before he could say anything he was taken by surprise when the drill teacher pointed directly to him.

'I'm sure Barry here would forgive me if I steal a fellow music lover for a couple of hours. What do you say, Barry?'

'Eh…' He tried to find a reason to object, but couldn't come up with anything. He caught Grace's eye and realised she had been following the conversation. Grace nodded her head and mouthed the words, 'Say yes.'

Barry's mind was racing, caught between trying to find an objection and going with Grace's suggestion. Because he knew at once what Grace had in mind. If Mr Pawlek was with his mother, they could enter his house and open the locked press. But he didn't want his mother to be alone with Pawlek, no matter how well it suited their break-in plans. In the end the decision was taken out of his hands.

'It would be a lovely night out for you, Ellen,' said Grandma. 'Sure I'll be there if Barry wants anything.'

'Well, if you're sure,' said Mum. 'Is that OK, Barry, just for one night?'

It would look suspicious now if he objected, so Barry tried to sound casual. 'Yes, it's fine, Mum.'

'Excellent,' said Mr Pawlek. 'The concert is at eight. Shall I call for you at say, seven fifteen?'

That would be fine,' said Mum. 'And thank you, Mr Pawlek, it's very considerate of you.'

'My pleasure. Well, until then. Ladies, gentlemen,' he said politely, making his goodbyes.

The others said their farewells, and as they did so Barry looked at Grace. She discreetly gave him a thumbs-up sign, and Barry nodded back. He knew that Grace was excited, and that an opportunity had presented itself. He realised too that his own heart was pounding. But he couldn't fool himself. His heart wasn't racing from excitement, but from fear.

CHAPTER TWENTY

'That was a brilliant film last night,' said Grace.

'Yeah, it was good,' answered Barry.

'And The Three Stooges are gas – I was still smiling when I got into bed!'

Grace and Barry were crossing Viking Place, the morning sunlight hazy as they made their way to call for Charlie on the way to sports camp.

'The Three Stooges are good, but Mum and I prefer the Marx Brothers.'

'Your ma is great fun,' said Grace. 'And dead generous. It was really nice of her to bring us to the pictures.'

On Sunday evening Mrs Malone had taken Barry, Grace and Charlie to the local cinema, the Broadway on Manor Street. She had paid for everyone's tickets and bought each of them an ice pop.

Barry nodded. 'She's sound, all right. But…'

'What?'

'I'm worried…'

'About her going out tonight with Mr Pawlek?'

'Yeah.'

'She'll be fine.'

Barry looked at Grace, concern etched on his face. 'He could be a Nazi!'

'But he's only bringing her to a concert. He's not going to harm her there.'

'He might get information out of her. About the aircraft factory.'

'Well, if we're wrong, and he's innocent, that won't matter,' said Grace.

'But we don't think he's innocent.'

'It still won't matter. Because then we'll be turning him over to the police.'

Barry continued to look worried, and Grace tried to raise his spirits.

'This is our chance, Barry,' she said. 'They'll be at the concert tonight for hours. It's perfect.'

'Not perfect. We could still be seen climbing the wall.'

'But not by Mr Pawlek. And we have to get into that locked press. You said it yourself.'

'I know. I just wish Mum wasn't involved.'

Grace felt sympathetic. If it were Ma she would be just as concerned as Barry was. But Mrs Malone had accepted the invitation to the concert, and neither she nor Barry could change that.

'I know how you must feel,' she said gently. 'But she's seeing him, whether we break in or not.'

Barry thought for a moment, then nodded slowly. 'You're right, I'm being stupid.'

'Not stupid.'

'Dithering then. And we can't dither.'

They turned into Norseman Place, and Barry stopped before they reached Charlie's house. 'OK, then, we do it tonight.'

'Sure?'

'Certain.'

'Right,' said Grace, nervous but at the same time excited at the idea. 'Tonight it is.'

The evening sunshine filled the room with warmth and mellow golden light, but it wasn't just the heat that was making Barry perspire. He breathed out deeply to calm himself, then wiped the thin film of perspiration from his forehead.

He had followed Grace over the wall of Mr Pawlek's garden once more, this time with a rucksack on his back, then Grace slipped the catch on the window and they entered the house and made for the living room. Barry pulled back the curtain on the alcove and, as he had expected, the padlock on the press was still there.

Grace went straight to work on trying to pick the lock. She was using a small flexible piece from a metal spring that Barry had got from his father's old toolbox, which was kept under the stairs in Grandma's. Not wanting to put Grace under pressure, Barry had stood back to let her at it, even though he found it hard to cope with standing there doing nothing.

He had felt deeply uneasy when Mr Pawlek had called to the

house for Mum, but had put on a good front, actually going so far as to say that he envied them hearing 'Rhapsody in Blue' being played live. Apart from suspecting Mr Pawlek of being an enemy agent, it was a little strange to see his mother going out for the evening with a man other than Dad. He wondered if the same thought would have occurred to Grandma. Mum was, after all, married to her son. But he suspected that Grandma – just like Mum – simply saw it as two music fans availing of an opportunity. And of course Grandma regarded Mr Pawlek as a perfect gentleman, who could be counted on to act accordingly.

Barry had waited about ten minutes after Mum and Mr Pawlek left before calling for Grace and making his way here. Which meant that they should have plenty of time before the concert ended and Mr Pawlek returned home. Even so, Barry felt really on edge as Grace worked on the lock. Supposing a neighbour had seen them scaling the wall and had told the police? It was one thing claiming you had trespassed into a garden to retrieve a ball, but going into the house itself was breaking and entering. *Come on!* he thought, as Grace wiggled the spring in the lock to no avail.

He forced himself to say nothing for what felt like ages, then eventually he couldn't contain himself. 'How long did your granddad say it would take?'

'He didn't say an exact time,' answered Grace, without looking up from what she was doing.

'He must have given you some idea!'

'He said you needed patience, and luck.'

'We can't hang around much longer, Grace, you've been trying for ages.'

Grace looked up at him briefly. 'I'm doing my best!'

'I know. But we have to get into that press.'

Grace had gone back to working on the lock, but now she breathed out in resignation. 'All right then,' she said, removing the spring. 'All right, do it your way.'

'Good try, Grace,' he said.

'But it didn't work. So let's do it your way.'

Barry nodded, then reached nervously into his rucksack.

Grace stepped back, disappointed that her efforts to open the lock had failed. It would have been exciting to get the lever in the lock to click open. It would have been a better tactic, too, because then if there was nothing incriminating in the press they could have relocked it without Mr Pawlek knowing. Still, no point worrying about that now. And besides, she still believed that they *would* find something.

She watched as Barry drew closer to the lock. He had found a bolt-cutter in his father's old toolbox, and was going to try to cut the metal neck of the lock.

Barry placed the teeth of the bolt cutter on either side of the metal band. Grace held her breath. If they were wrong and Mr Pawlek was an innocent man, then there would be no disguising a snapped lock. And if Mr Pawlek reported a break-in, and the police questioned the neighbours, she and Barry might well be identified as the culprits.

It was too awful to dwell on, so she swallowed hard and tried to put it from her mind. Instead, she watched as Barry closed the arms of the bolt cutter. To Grace's dismay it didn't cut through the lock.

'I thought you said it cuts through all kinds of metal?' she said.

'It does. But I think the lock is steel – it's really tough.'

Barry tried again, pressing with all his might to make the bolt cutter shear through the metal. Despite Barry's face going red with the effort, the lock didn't snap.

'Here, why don't we both do it?' said Grace.

Barry hesitated, looking uncomfortable with his failure.

Grace sensed that his pride was at stake, but she couldn't bear the thought of coming this far and not succeeding, so she looked him in the eye and spoke bluntly. 'Come on, Barry, this isn't about how strong you are. We have to snap that lock.'

He seemed to weigh this up for a moment, then nodded. 'OK.'

Grace took one arm of the bolt cutter and Barry the other, and together they closed the tool on the resisting neck of the lock. They both pressed hard, but still the lock held. Eventually they had to breathe out and let go.

'Damn!' said Barry.

'Let's try again,' urged Grace.

'All right.'

They applied the bolt cutter again. Grace strained hard, and this time she felt the tool biting into the metal. She pushed with all of her strength, but still they couldn't snap all the way through the steel, and after a moment they had to admit defeat again.

'We made some headway there,' said Barry, looking thoughtful.

'I was using every ounce of my strength,' answered Grace. 'I can't push any harder.'

'I've an idea,' said Barry. 'Know what leverage is?'

'No.'

'It's where you get extra power by using something solid as a tool. If we brace ourselves against the walls of the alcove, we can use the walls for leverage.'

'How?'

'The alcove is narrow, so you wedge your shoulder against one side and jam your feet up against the other side. I do the same from the opposite direction, then we both push with all our might, pressing back against the walls.'

'OK,' said Grace, immediately moving and jamming herself into the alcove the way that Barry had said.

Barry quickly did the same, then they raised the bolt cutter again. Grace pushed hard, her shoulder hurting from where it pressed back into the wall, but she did feel she was exerting more power this time.

'Come on!' said Barry, 'Come on!'

They both pressed, faces straining, then suddenly there was a snap and the lock fell to the floor.

'Yes!' cried Grace. She lowered her feet from the wall.

Barry reached for the handle of the press. 'Right' he said, 'let's see what he's hiding!'

* * *

Barry felt his hand trembling as he opened the door of the press. He was going to feel pretty stupid if the press was empty. Or if it contained something that Mr Pawlek regarded as valuable enough to lock away, but which had nothing to do with spying. *Too late now...*

He pulled the door open and looked in. The press wasn't empty. Resting on a shelf was a compact looking suitcase, and to the right of the case were two small boxes. There was nothing else in the cupboard, and Barry moved at once to take out the suitcase.

It was heavy enough for its size, and Barry placed it on the table, his pulses racing. He paused a moment, and Grace impatiently indicated the clips that allowed the case to be opened.

'Come on, Barry!' she said.

He reached out and undid first one clip, then the other. He took a deep breath, then opened the lid of the case.

'Oh my God!' said Grace.

It was a radio transmitter, with leads attached and a key for tapping out messages in Morse code.

'I knew it!' said Grace. 'I just knew it!'

'Yeah,' answered Barry.

She looked at him, her expression surprised. 'You don't sound pleased.'

Barry looked at the radio, his mind a whirl of mixed emotions. 'I'm glad we got proof. But part of me…part of me didn't really want him to be a spy.'

'I know what you mean. He *is* pretty likeable. But then again that only shows you what a snake he really is. It's all a front.'

Barry nodded grimly 'Yeah, you're right. And now that we know, we have to stop him.'

'So what will we do?'

'We have to go to the police, tonight.'

'And tell them we broke in here?' said Grace nervously.

'They won't care about that if it means catching a spy.'

'I hope not.'

'They won't, Grace. This is way bigger than breaking in. He's been *spying*. People get executed for that.'

'Right.'

'Let's check the other boxes. The more we know, the better.'

'OK,' agreed Grace, as Barry turned back to the open press.

He took out the first box. It was square and wooden, and Barry quickly opened the top.

'Gosh!' said Grace.

Barry swallowed hard. Then he reached into the box and took out a lethal looking pistol and a shoulder holster. The gun smelt lightly of oil and was spotlessly clean, suggesting to Barry a weapon that was well maintained.

'This is getting scary,' said Grace.

'Yeah,' agreed Barry, 'but if we move fast the police can set a trap. They can lie in wait at Grandma's – he's sure to see Mum home before coming here. And once he's dropped Mum off they could arrest him while he's unarmed.'

'Good plan,' said Grace, 'But are you sure–'

'Shush!' said Barry cutting her off.

'What?'

'I thought I heard a noise.'

They both stood silently for a moment, listening intently. Then Barry's stomach contracted in terror as he heard the front door opening and closing, followed by the sound of footsteps coming down the hall.

Paralysed by fear, Grace stood unmoving for a moment. The footsteps grew nearer, then Grace sprang forward and ran towards the window. The only door in the room led out into the hallway, so the one means of escape lay in climbing out the window into the garden.

Her hands were trembling, but Grace managed to undo the catch and pull open the window sash. She heard the footsteps stopping outside in the hall. Fighting back a sense of panic, she began to clamber up onto the window ledge. Before she could exit from the window, however, the door to the room burst open and she heard Mr Pawlek's voice. He cried out what sounded like a swear word in a foreign language.

Grace forced herself not to look back, but instead swung up on the window ledge, pulling back the net curtains so she could jump down the short drop into the garden.

She sensed Mr Pawlek racing across the room, and she desperately clambered to swing her legs around. Terrified at being caught, she jumped just as he reached her.

It was only a few feet down into the garden, but she never landed. Instead she felt herself being yanked backwards. Mr Pawlek had caught the shoulders of her dress and he roughly pulled her back in over the window ledge and into the room, slamming the window shut after him.

'Grace!' he said, startled on discovering her identity. 'What the hell are you doing?!'

Grace's mind raced frantically as she tried to come up with an explanation. She noticed that there was no sign of Barry. But the curtains were drawn on the alcove. *He had to be hiding there.* 'I was...'

'You were what?' demanded Pawlek when she faltered. 'You were what?!' he repeated, grabbing Grace by the arm and pulling her closer.

'You're hurting me!' she cried.

But Pawlek's eyes were cold and angry, and he maintained his grip for a moment, then shook her arm hard before letting go.

'You've no idea what pain is,' he said roughly. 'But you will if you don't tell me what you were doing.'

Grace had never seen him like this, and the change in his manner was really chilling.

Fearing for her life, she found her imagination kicking in, and she tried to make herself sound convincing as she answered. 'I...I broke in to steal money. My ma is poor, and you...you seemed well-off, so I thought you might have spare cash.'

Pawlek's eyes burned into hers as he drew closer. 'Lying little bitch!' he said, then he slapped Grace across the face.

She staggered backwards. The blow hadn't been full force, but she hadn't been expecting it and it hurt her. But with the pain came anger, and she forced herself not to give him the satisfaction of seeing her cry. She saw the radio set with its Morse code key on the table and she realised that Pawlek must have seen it too – and there was no mistaking the significance of a secret radio in wartime.

'Don't lie to me,' said Pawlek, his tone low and threatening. 'I know you didn't break in to steal money.'

'If you know, why are you asking me?' said Grace.

'Answer the question! Why did you come here?'

Grace stared at him defiantly. Pawlek approached her and raised his hand threateningly. 'I'll only ask once more. Why did you come here?'

'We wanted the proof!' she said. 'That you're a spy! That you're a Nazi!'

Pawlek gave no reaction to the accusation. Instead he looked at her searchingly and said, *'We?'*

'Myself and Barry,' answered Grace, improvising. 'But he got away. He'll be telling the police right how. And you're going to be locked up – if they don't hang you!'

'Really?'

'Yes, really!'

'Just one problem. There are two ways out of this room. The door I came in, and the window. And you'd only just opened the window, hadn't you?'

Grace tried to think up a convincing reply, but Pawlek spoke again.

'So unless Barry can walk through walls, he's still here. Let's see what's behind the curtain, shall we?'

Barry stood stock still in the alcove. He knew that he was going to be discovered as soon as Pawlek pulled back the curtain. His heart felt like it would explode in his chest, and he could feel his knees trembling. He breathed in deeply to try to calm himself, but he still started when Pawlek suddenly pulled aside the curtain. Pawlek was surprised, too. The drill teacher might have been expecting Barry to be hiding in the alcove; he hadn't been expecting him to have a pistol. And it was pointing directly at him.

Barry held the weapon he had taken from the wooden box, using both hands to aim it at Pawlek's chest.

'Put your hands on your head!' ordered Barry, making sure to keep out of lunging distance of the teacher.

Pawlek just stared at him.

'Do it! Now!' said Barry, tightening his fingers on the trigger.

'Put the gun down, you snooping brat, and maybe I won't give you a thrashing!'

'Shut your mouth, you Nazi pig!' snapped Barry angrily. 'And get your hands on your head!' He saw a flash of anger in Pawlek's eyes, then to his surprise the drill teacher gave a cold smile.

'*Get your hands on your head*? You've watched too many silly films. Spoiled by that stupid mother of yours.'

Barry felt a stab of anxiety. 'If you've hurt my mother I'll blow your brains out!' he said.

'Your mother hurt herself. Sprained her ankle on the kerb and had to go home. Worse luck for you.'

'Worse luck for you, you mean. I have the gun – don't think I won't use it.'

'You won't be able.'

Barry controlled his anger and took careful aim so as to hit Pawlek in the heart.

'Won't I? I've seen what your planes did to Liverpool. My friend's sister was blown to smithereens. She was only sixteen. So if you think I won't shoot, just try your luck.'

'Bravely spoken. But you don't know much about guns, do you?' said Pawlek, and something in his confident tone made Barry fearful.

'First of all, that gun's not loaded. And even if it was, you never took off the safety catch.'

Barry felt a stab of panic and he looked down to locate the safety catch. In the instant that he took his eye off the drill teacher, Pawlek sprang at him. Barry flicked the catch and pulled the trigger, hoping that Pawlek was bluffing about the weapon being unloaded. In that instant the teacher landed on him, the other man's momentum knocking Barry painfully back against the door of the press. Worse than the pain was the realisation that the trigger had clicked on an empty chamber.

Pawlek grabbed the wrist of his gun hand in a numbing grip, then snatched the weapon from Barry's fingers with his other hand. Barry tried to struggle, but he reeled backwards again when Pawlek smacked him hard in the face, knocking him to the ground.

Barry began to rise shakily to this feet, his face stinging from the blow.

'Are you OK?' said Grace, her own voice wavering with fear, as she stooped to help him up.

'Yes,' he answered, determined to show no weakness in front of his enemy. He saw that Pawlek had taken the other box from the press and was loading the pistol with bullets stored in the box.

'Now,' said Pawlek, as he finished loading the weapon and pointed it at Barry and Grace. 'Now you've given me a problem. So we have to dispose of two people who were too nosey. But you should have thought of that before you interfered, shouldn't you?'

Grace struggled against her bonds, but it was useless. Pawlek had improvised effectively, quickly tying herself and Barry to kitchen chairs with heavy twine from a drawer, then gagging them with tea towels tied tightly around their mouths and knotted at the back.

She had never seen him angry before, but she and Barry had caused him a major problem. His carefully maintained cover as a Polish national was blown now, and he would either have to go into hiding or flee the country.

Unless…she didn't want to think about it, but there *was* one other possibility. If he were to kill herself and Barry, then maybe he could continue as a spy. It was a horrifying thought that really scared her. But Grace tried to reassure herself that Pawlek couldn't be sure they hadn't shared their suspicions about him with anyone else. He would be taking a huge risk to try and carry on, especially as the police would undoubtedly question him as part of the massive enquiry that would take place if two children from his sports club went missing.

Besides, if he wanted to kill them they would surely be dead by now. Instead of which he had tied them up, told them that he would be back shortly, and warned them not to try anything. But then again if he really did mean to kill them, wouldn't he want to do it someplace remote, rather than in his own kitchen?

Grace felt a stab of panic at the thought, but forced it down. *Be logical.* What would you do if you were in his shoes? *Have a back-up plan and use it.* Every spy ran the risk of being exposed and having to flee. That meant he would have someplace where he could hide while waiting to be rescued. Maybe a little cottage near some remote stretch of coastline where a submarine could secretly pick him up. But he *would* have someplace lined up.

Grace considered how he might get there. Mr Pawlek didn't have a car at his house, so maybe he was gone now to collect one that he had hidden. Or more likely, to steal one. Either way, it would make sense for him to buy time and cover his trail by taking her and Barry with him. And once he had safely organised his getaway there was no gain for him in killing or injuring two children. Or was she kidding herself? The world was at war and millions of people were being killed. Maybe to Pawlek two more lives would mean nothing. The thought terrified her, and she tried to force it from her mind as she sat tied to the chair, waiting for their captor to return.

Barry's face ached from where Pawlek had hit him. And, with his hands and feet tied to the chair, he couldn't rub it to ease the pain. Ever since he had heard the sound of Pawlek at the front door Barry had struggled to cope with his fear. Now he felt angry, too, and he gave way to his anger, sensing instinctively that it would be healthier to be angry with Pawlek than to be afraid of him.

He had to fight back, he just had to. But how? Pawlek had left the house, so now was the time to act. But what could he do, when he wasn't able to move from the chair? *Think, Barry,* he ordered himself. And then it struck him. *He* couldn't move from the chair, but the *chair itself* was moveable. Barry's feet were resting on the floor, his ankles tied to the legs of the chair. But supposing he took his weight on the soles of his feet, then launched himself upwards and forward a couple of inches? Could he bunny-hop across the carpeted room? He tried it, and saw Grace looking at him enquiringly. He couldn't explain to her what he was doing, with both of them gagged. He wasn't even sure himself. But he *had* moved forward several inches.

If he were to make his way to the window, could he smash it somehow? And then what? He couldn't count on the sound of one pane being broken alerting the neighbours. And, being gagged, he still couldn't call out for help. Could he use the jagged glass of a broken window pane to rub against the heavy twine that was binding him? He looked again at the window and his heart sank. The window pane was too high; he would never be able to get his wrist up to the glass. But now that the idea of somehow cutting the twine had arisen he looked around the room with fresh eyes. A knife, a scissors, some kind of sharp object might be available. His hands were tied low down behind him, to the back of the chair, but his fingers were free to grasp an object if he could get near enough to something suitable. But this was the living room, not the kitchen, and as he looked around he saw no cutlery, no penknife, and no letter opener, nothing that would cut twine.

Barry scanned the room again, then his eyes fixed upon the fireplace. Because it was July a fire hadn't been lit in months, and down on the tiled fireplace surround there were two miniature glass vases. Red roses from the back garden had been placed in each vase, and Barry's hopes stirred.

Frantically bunny-hopping the chair, he made his way across the room to the fireplace. He continued until he was beside one of the vases. Sweat had formed on his forehead, but he ignored it, concentrating instead on extending his fingers to try to reach the stem of the small vase. The twine bit into his wrists painfully and he couldn't quite get his fingers to grasp the rim of the vase. Instead he tried bunny hopping sideways to get a little nearer to his target. The perspiration was now running into his eyes, but he blinked to clear his vision and concentrated on trying to grasp the vase. His fingers brushed against it and again the twine bit into his wrists. Ignoring the pain, he extended his fingers to full stretch and was rewarded by grasping the vase between his thumb and first finger.

He felt a surge of satisfaction and paused briefly for breath, allowing himself to think out his next move. The glass didn't have a lot of water in it, but he didn't want Pawlek to see any spillage. He manoeuvred his fingers so that his hand covered the top of the vase, then hopped sideways again around an armchair that had been placed in front of the fireplace. He had now reached an area of carpet between the armchair and the corner wall that couldn't be seen easily from most other parts of the room.

The gag was forcing Barry to breathe noisily through his nostrils and he paused again to get his breath. Then he managed to tilt the vase so that the flowers fell out and the water soaked into the carpet where it wouldn't be seen. He allowed the vase to slip from his fingers, getting it right up against the wall. Once more he bunny-hopped sideways, violently this time, smashing the edge of the chair against the vase and breaking it into pieces.

He felt a thrill, and looking across the room, caught Grace's eye. She nodded encouragingly, aware now, he reckoned, of what he was up to. Barry nodded back, then pressed his bound wrist down and outwards, fully extending his fingers and touching several pieces of broken glass. He wanted a piece that had a sharp edge, but was still big enough for him to hold firmly with his fingers while he tried to saw through the twine. He felt a couple of pieces but they were too small. Stretching his fingers further out, he came upon another piece about two inches long. *Perfect.*

Grasping the sliver of glass, he tried rubbing it against the thick twine. With his wrists bound it was hard to hold the glass at the right angle for sawing. This was going to take some time, he realised. His instincts were to get started, however long it might take to cut his bonds. But if Pawlek came back and found him over here, he would discover the flowers and the broken vase and the game would be up. No, better to bunny-hop back to where he had been. That way if he hadn't freed himself by the time Pawlek returned, the drill teacher probably wouldn't know what he had been up to, and he could hide the sliver of glass in his hand.

How long would it take to cut through the heavy twine? And how long was Pawlek likely to be gone? He didn't know, but every second might be precious, and so he wasted no more time wondering, and started back across the room.

CHAPTER TWENTY-ONE

Grace breathed in and out deeply, doing her best to stay calm. The sun was starting to sink, and as they drove along she saw glimpses of gorse-covered mountainside bathed in golden light. She was lying beside Barry on the floor in the back of a diesel-smelling van that she presumed Pawlek had stolen. They had been driving for a long time now, and Grace reckoned that they must be in some remote region of the Wicklow mountains. Was their captor taking them to some organised hideaway, or was he just waiting for darkness to fall before disposing of them, somewhere well off the beaten track? She prayed that he wasn't that ruthless. But if he was, then being frightened wasn't going to help. No, she told herself, she had to keep her wits about her, and be prepared to fight back if the chance arose.

She had suspected that they had a long journey ahead of them when Mr Pawlek had briefly untied herself and Barry, one at a time, and allowed them to use the toilet before leaving the house in Manor Street. Luckily, Barry had just started trying to fray the thick twine when Pawlek had returned, and the teacher hadn't noticed anything amiss with his bonds. After the toilet he had immediately retied their hands behind their backs, and Grace had wondered how he planned to transfer them, bound and gagged, and in broad daylight, to the vehicle parked outside the house.

But Pawlek was smart, and he had taken up the carpet from one of the bedrooms, wrapped Barry in it, and carried it out to the van on his shoulder, before coming back to do the same with Grace. Any passers-by would simply see a man moving a roll of carpet into a van. Meanwhile there was no way of crying out because of the gags. Pawlek had warned Barry that he would shoot Grace in the knee – a really painful wound, he said – if Barry kicked the side of the van or caused any kind of rumpus while Pawlek went back in for her, or indeed at any stage when they started driving. From the cold-blooded way that he said it, Grace believed him. Her stomach had tightened in fear at the threat, but obviously Barry believed it too and he had obeyed Pawlek and not tried to raise the alarm.

There were no windows in the back of the van, so Grace and Barry had been invisible to other motorists as they lay uncomfortably on the carpet that Pawlek had thrown onto the floor in the rear of the vehicle. They could see the back of Pawlek's head through the opening between the driver's seat and the interior of the van, but unless he turned around – which he only did from time to time – Pawlek couldn't see them.

It was the one advantage they had, and Grace's hopes rested on the fact that Barry had kept the sliver of glass wrapped in his fist, and then managed to cut through the twine binding his wrists. For the last few minutes he had been secretly trying to free her also. It was tricky work, what with the van bouncing on the mountain road and with Barry having to lie beside her as if his own hands were still tied, in case Pawlek turned around. If both of them had their hands free, they would have the element of surprise on their captor, though how they might use that against an armed adult she wasn't sure.

The road levelled out somewhat, and with the smoother ride she felt Barry getting a good rhythm going as he tried to saw through her bindings. But the light was slowly starting to fade, and she suspected that Pawlek wouldn't want to be driving in the dark. Which meant that Barry needed to cut through the twine as soon as possible. Trying to hold her wrists steady, she pushed back against the sliver of glass, desperately wishing for it to cut through her bonds.

Barry saw Pawlek turning around in the driver's seat and he immediately stopped sawing at Grace's bonds. He lay with his hands behind him as their captor glanced round to ensure that all was well in the rear of the van. Barry avoided eye-contact with Pawlek, and the teacher turned back to steering the vehicle, presumably satisfied that Grace and Barry were still in his power.

Barry waited a few seconds, then went straight back to working on the twine that secured Grace's wrists. He wasn't too far away from sawing right through, and he worked as fast as he could now, knowing that he couldn't make his move until Grace was free.

He felt the last strands beginning to shred, and he slowed down, not wanting to cut Grace when the glass sheared through the twine. He sawed gently, then suddenly there was no more resistance and he could see the relief in Grace's eyes as she brought her arms forward and rubbed her sore wrists.

Despite the fact that they were both still gagged, Barry immediately put a finger to his lips, for fear that in her relief Grace might sigh or make some noise that would alert Pawlek. Grace nodded in understanding, and only then did Barry undo the knot behind his head to remove his gag. Grace followed his example, then Barry leaned in close to whisper in her ear. The noise of the engine reverberated through the vehicle, but still he kept his voice as soft as possible. 'When I make my move, brace yourself, then jump out the back door. OK?'

Grace looked at him, her eyes wide, and he hoped she wasn't going to panic. Instead, she nodded in agreement.

Barry felt his hands and knees trembling, and he breathed out, trying to keep his nerves under control. He had planned this out over the course of the long drive, and he knew what was required. *Act as soon as possible after freeing Grace and before Pawlek looks around again.*

But for maximum impact he wanted to strike while Pawlek was negotiating a bend, and right now the mountain road was running fairly straight. Was it worth the risk of waiting for the perfect moment? Pawlek might not look around again for five minutes. Or he might look in five seconds. And if he saw that Barry and

Grace had freed themselves they would lose the crucial element of surprise.

Barry bit his lip, not sure what to do. Next moment the van slowed slightly as Pawlek braked to take a sharp bend. Barry swallowed hard. *This was his chance.* He willed himself to action, but hesitated a moment, scared of what needed to be done, and what would happen to him if it went wrong.

The van continued to curve around the bend and Barry knew that if he hesitated any longer this opportunity would be gone. Steeling himself, he grabbed the twine that had been used to bind his wrists, then raised himself in the back of the van, spreading his legs wide apart to keep his balance. Suddenly he sprang forward, looping the twine over Pawlek's head. He pulled hard on the cord, digging his knees into the back of the driver's seat and hauling the unsuspecting Pawlek backwards by the neck. The teacher cried out in pain and shock. His hands flew up from the steering wheel as he tried to loosen the cord that was biting into his neck. Barry pulled hard on the twine and braced himself as the teacher lost control of the vehicle and the van drove off the road.

Grace was flung against the side wall of the van as it bounced wildly up and down over the uneven mountain terrain. Pawlek had completely lost control of the van, which was slewing sideways but gradually slowing. Grace could see that Pawlek had forced one hand under the twine, relieving some of the pressure on his neck, and with the other hand he was flailing wildly behind him, trying to strike Barry, who was still hauling on the string. The teacher was pulled back at an awkward angle, however, and Barry had evaded the blows.

Just then the van must have hit a rock, because there was a crashing sound and the vehicle shuddered to a jarring stop. Everyone was thrown forward, and Grace landed against the back of the front passenger seat. Pawlek and Barry were flung forward, too and Barry lost his grip on the twine. Grace saw Pawlek's forehead bang against the windscreen, then Barry screamed at her.

'Go, Grace, go!'

They both scuttled to the back door of the van. Barry pulled the release handle, and they tumbled out into the fading light of the summer evening. They were on a remote, sloping mountainside with bogland below them, the water-filled bog holes reflecting the golden rays of the setting sun, and the air sweet and pure. At another time it would have been beautiful, but Grace was too frightened to appreciate the scenery.

She scrambled forward, ahead of Barry, just as Pawlek spilled out of the driver's door. He looked disoriented from the blow his head had taken against the windscreen, but he reacted instinctively and made a grab for Grace. She screamed and ducked beneath his outstretched arm. Pawlek lost his balance and, desperate to gain any advantage, Grace reached out and pushed him hard.

Pawlek fell heavily down the hillside. Grace could see that he was heading for one of the bog holes. He grasped desperately at ferns but couldn't arrest his fall, and he landed with a splash in the squelching brown water of the bog hole. Grace watched in horror as he sank, despite his frantic efforts to pull himself out. Pawlek grasped again at the ferns, but they came away in his hand as he desperately tried to halt his immersion.

Partly relieved, partly horrified, Grace expected to see him go under. When the water was about halfway up his chest, however, he stopped sinking. Obviously gaining heart, Pawlek made a huge effort to free himself, but it soon became clear that the oozing mud and peaty water of the bog hole were holding him fast, and that he wouldn't be able to gain the purchase needed to pull himself out.

'Let's go, Grace!' said Barry and, realising that Pawlek wasn't going to drown, Grace turned away. She was just starting the climb back to the road when a shot rang out, striking a rock immediately in front of her.

'Don't move, or the next one's in your back!'

Grace stopped, terrified. And mixed with the terror of being shot was fury at herself. *Why hadn't she run as soon as she had the chance?!* She could see that Barry was nearer to the road, but he too had stopped.

'Turn around,' said Pawlek. 'Turn around!'

Grace did as she was told and she saw Barry also turning.

'Come closer, Barry!'

'No.'

'Do as I say if you don't want your friend shot!' called Pawlek, still up past his waist in water but with the pistol that he had taken from the hidden shoulder holster pointed directly at her.

Grace tried not to flinch, but there was a wild look in Pawlek's eyes, and she didn't doubt that he was capable of carrying out the threat.

'You won't shoot Grace,' Barry called back, his voice surprisingly cool.

'What, you think I can't kill a child? Thousands of children have died in this war, millions maybe. What's one more?'

'If you shoot Grace I'll be gone before you get off any more shots. I'm pretty much out of pistol range as it is. And if you kill Grace I swear I'll let you die here. There's been hardly any traffic on this road – you won't be rescued. You'll drown in that bog hole or die of exposure.'

'Then two people will have died pointlessly. But do as I tell you, and no-one dies. I had no plans to kill you or Grace. I was just going to leave you somewhere remote so I'd be long gone when you raised the alarm.'

Grace really wanted to believe this.

'There's a tow-rope in the back of the van,' said Pawlek. 'Get it and tie one end to the hazel tree there. Then throw the other end to me so I can haul myself out. Do that and nobody dies.'

Barry said nothing in reply, and Grace saw the impatience in Pawlek's eyes. 'Tell your stubborn friend you want to live, Grace!'

Grace considered this. As it was, with Barry pretty much out of accurate pistol range, he was safe. Could she ask him to risk his life by getting a rope to rescue Pawlek? The spy would still have the gun, and he might break his word and kill both of them. On the other hand, he might *keep* his word, and she really didn't want to die.

'Tell him, Grace!' ordered Pawlek, cocking the pistol. 'Tell him if you want to live!'

Grace swallowed hard, not knowing what to do.

'She doesn't have to,' said Barry. 'I'll get the rope.'

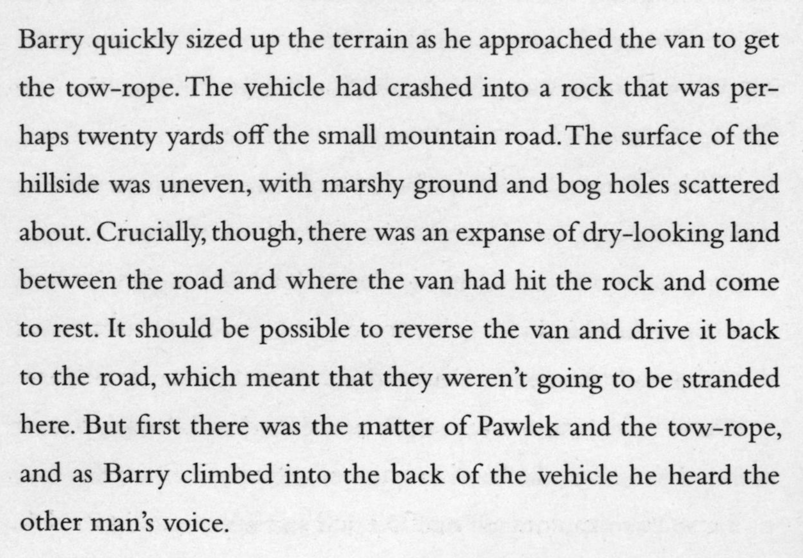

Barry quickly sized up the terrain as he approached the van to get the tow-rope. The vehicle had crashed into a rock that was perhaps twenty yards off the small mountain road. The surface of the hillside was uneven, with marshy ground and bog holes scattered about. Crucially, though, there was an expanse of dry-looking land between the road and where the van had hit the rock and come to rest. It should be possible to reverse the van and drive it back to the road, which meant that they weren't going to be stranded here. But first there was the matter of Pawlek and the tow-rope, and as Barry climbed into the back of the vehicle he heard the other man's voice.

'Hurry up!'

'All right, I'm coming,' cried Barry, as he located a long, tightly bound rope that was wedged behind the spare wheel. He climbed out of the van and made his way down the steep slope to where Pawlek was still trapped in the bog hole, and still with the pistol aimed at Grace. Barry looked carefully to see if Pawlek had sunk any further. The mud and water were about chest-high – enough to keep him trapped but not enough to drown him.

'Come on!' said Pawlek.

Barry had the rope in his hand, ready for throwing, but something stopped him.

'What are you waiting for?' demanded Pawlek.

'We've only your word you'll do what you say,' said Barry.

'I will. There's no gain in killing you.'

'Isn't there?'

'Look,' said Pawlek, obviously making an effort to sound reasonable, 'I'm going to be out of the country pretty soon. You saw the radio, I used it to call a submarine. I'll be gone after dark. I just planned to leave you two in the wilds. By the time you walk to civilisation, I'll be long gone. But we'll all be alive.'

Barry thought hard, trying to gauge if he could really trust him.

'Otherwise,' said Pawlek, his voice hardening again, 'Grace will die. And probably you too. You're nearer now, and I'm a good shot.'

Barry's mind was racing as he continued weighing up how much of this might be bluff and how much might be true.

'I give you my word as an officer and a gentleman,' said Pawlek. 'Throw me the rope and we all walk away unharmed. Otherwise...'

Barry looked at Grace. He could see that she was really frightened and that she believed Pawlek's threat to kill her. And yet she didn't beg for mercy. Nor did she try to sway him to give Pawlek the rope. He was impressed by her bravery and in that moment he knew that he couldn't risk letting Pawlek shoot her.

'All right,' said Barry resignedly. Then he tied one end of the rope to the hazel tree and threw the other end to Pawlek, hoping this wasn't the biggest mistake of his life.

Grace watched carefully as Pawlek awkwardly wrapped the rope around himself, feeding it under his armpits. She saw that he was going to tie it in a loop and then use it to pull himself out. So far he had kept the pistol trained on her, but to tie a knot he would have to use two hands – which would make aiming the gun very difficult. If she was going to make a run for it, that would be her opportunity. But it was risky. He might regain his aim quickly and shoot her. Whereas if they went along with his scheme, the worst that they faced was a very long walk in the mountains. *If he was telling the truth, that is.* But even if he was, they would still be letting a Nazi spy escape. *And if he wasn't telling the truth?* If he decided that he wanted no witnesses, what was to stop him shooting them both and heading off to his submarine rendezvous?

Maybe it would be better to take a risk than to rely on the word of a spy – *a man who told lies for a living.* Grace pondered it a moment more then suddenly made her mind up. She stood staring into space as Pawlek experimented with the rope. She tried to look dejected, wanting to give Pawlek the impression that she was frightened into submission, and therefore no threat to him.

From the corner of her eye she could see that Pawlek was concentrating on the rope, and when he moved his gun hand to tighten the loop, Grace didn't hesitate. She dived to the ground.

'Run, Barry, run!' she cried.

Without rising or looking up she rolled away at speed over the rough ground, desperately willing herself to get out of Pawlek's line of fire. Two shots rang out, deafening in the still of the evening, and Grace saw a final blur of the setting sun as she fell backwards into the ferns.

Barry looked in horror as Pawlek fired the pistol at Grace. He saw his friend fall back into the ferns and he was consumed with anger. Forgetting all thoughts of escaping, he reacted on instinct, grabbed a fist-sized granite rock and ran towards Pawlek. His momentum took him down the hill at speed but what happened next seemed to unfold almost in slow motion. Pawlek was still gripping the rope with one hand and trying to swing round to aim the pistol with the other. Before he could get a shot off, Barry had closed the gap between them. He reached the edge of the bog hole and flung the rock, catching Pawlek solidly on the head. There was a sickening thud, and Pawlek fell backwards into the bog hole, the pistol flying from his hand, with only the rope that was looped under his arms keeping his unconscious form from falling forward and sinking down in the squelching mud and water.

Barry immediately scooped up the pistol from where it had landed on the ground. He swung around and aimed it at Pawlek. He felt his finger tightening on the trigger, but the other man was clearly unconscious, and Barry hesitated to shoot him in cold blood. Instead, he lowered the pistol and started towards the ferns where he had seen Grace falling.

'Grace!' he cried, terrified of what he might find, 'Grace!'

'Here! Over here!'

He swiftly moved through the ferns, then came upon her. She looked shaken from having tumbled backwards down the hillside but she didn't seem to have any obvious injuries as she sat up gingerly.

'Are you OK?' he asked, hunkering down beside her.

Grace nodded. 'I'm fine.'

Barry felt a flood of relief that Pawlek's shots had missed her.

'You got the gun,' she said.

'It flew out of his hand when I hit him with a rock. He's out cold.'

'Oh thank God, Barry. I was so scared.'

'Me too,' he answered with a wry grin. 'Me too.'

Grace tried for a smile in return, then instead reached out and hugged Barry for a moment.

He hugged her back, relieved that they had outwitted so

dangerous an enemy, then he rose to his feet and held out his hand to help her up. 'Sure you're OK?'

'Just a few scrapes.'

They made their way back to the bog hole where Pawlek was slumped unconscious. A trickle of blood had run down his forehead, but the rope tied to the hazel tree prevented him from slumping under the surface.

'What do we do now?' asked Grace.

'The bumper on the van is caved in, but the wheel looks all right. I'll push the bumper out with a bit of wood, then I reckon I can drive the van back up onto the road.'

'Right.'

'The sun is going down over there,' said Barry pointing. 'So if we try to drive in the opposite direction it will bring us east, and eventually we'll reach the coast.'

'What about Mr Pawlek?'

'Looks like he won't be making his submarine,' said Barry, unable to keep the bitterness from his tone.

Grace looked at him. 'Are you saying…are you saying we just leave him here?'

'He tried to shoot you, Grace. He was ready to kill both of us.'

'Even if he was. You said yourself, he could die of exposure out here.'

Barry thought of all the innocent civilians in Liverpool who had been killed because of people like Mr Pawlek. Would one death in retaliation be so awful?

'Barry?' said Grace softly. 'Are you really saying we should just leave him?'

'He's a Nazi, Grace.'

'I know,' she answered. 'But we're not.'

Barry thought back to what Mum had said about British values. And how the best way to win against the likes of Hitler was to stay true to normal, decent values despite the depths to which the Nazis stooped. He stood lost in thought for a moment as the twilight deepened, then he turned to Grace. 'OK, then,' he said. 'We'll tie him hand and foot, and take him back as a prisoner.'

He handed Grace the pistol. 'You hold onto this, I'll go and free the mudguard. Then we'll tie the rope to the back bumper and use the van to haul him out. All right?'

'Fine.'

'OK,' said Barry his spirits lifting again in the knowledge that they were doing the right thing. 'Let's bring back a prisoner!'

Grace was impressed by how Barry handled the van. First he freed the mudguard like he had said, then he proved how well his Uncle George had taught him to drive, manoeuvring the vehicle up the hillside, with just enough revving of the engine to slowly pull the prostrate form of Mr Pawlek forward and out of the bog hole.

'OK Barry, that will do!' Grace cried. She saw him stopping the vehicle, the engine still idling as he got out to untie the rope from the bumper. She knelt beside the unconscious drill teacher, who looked a mess with his bloodied head and filthy, mud-sodden clothes.

Grace undid the rope that had been looped under his arms, drawing it up over his head. Suddenly Pawlek grabbed her left arm, and Grace screamed in shock. She had put the gun down on the ground, thinking herself in no danger from a man who was injured and unconscious. *But she shouldn't have underestimated someone as cunning as Pawlek!* And now his eyes were wide open and he was lunging for the gun. Grace felt a surge of anger. It was partly directed at herself, but mostly at Pawlek, whom she could have left stranded in the bog hole. Instead she had behaved decently, and this was her reward. She couldn't let him get to the gun, but she knew that he was stronger than her and would overpower her before Barry could join in. She had one chance, and one chance only, and with very ounce of her strength she drove her right fist at her opponent, aiming for his wounded head. She was rewarded with a roar of agony as Pawlek clutched his bloodied head wound, then Grace rolled away from him and scooped up the gun.

She could see Barry approaching at speed, but this was her fight, and she held the gun with both hands and pointed it at Pawlek.

'Don't,' he cried, 'please.'

Grace aimed at his chest. She was furious at Pawlek for tricking her, and he was a highly dangerous Nazi who couldn't be trusted not to try something else.

'Please,' he said again. 'Don't shoot. Please.'

Grace hesitated. She looked at his swollen forehead and the blood trickling again into his eye, and her fury abated a little. 'OK,' she said finally in a voice still cold with anger, 'you lie face down on the ground with your hands behind your back. Do it, now!'

Pawlek obeyed her.

Grace came up behind him and pressed the gun against the back of his neck. 'Barry will tie you, hands and feet, and if you try anything I'll shoot you. One more trick, one wrong move, and I'll empty this gun into you! Understand?!'

'Yes.'

'Certain?'

'Yes!'

'You think you're so smart, don't you? How does it feel to be beaten by a couple of kids?'

Pawlek had no answer, and Grace kept the gun pressed to the back of his neck but looked over at her friend and nodded.

'OK, Barry. Like you said, let's bring home a prisoner.'

Night had fallen now, and Barry felt excited as he drove east, the van's headlights picking out the twists and turns on the mountain roads. Even as he concentrated on the route, he couldn't help but savour the thrill of what they had done.

Pawlek was securely bound hand and foot in the back of the van. Once he had been helplessly trussed up and hauled into the rear of the vehicle, Grace had bathed his head wound and applied a makeshift bandage. *Grace.* The more he thought about her the more he realised that she had been brilliant tonight. She had been brave, and tough, and cool when it mattered most. Though, really, he shouldn't have been surprised at any of that, because she had been a cool customer – and a great friend – right from the start.

Now the van rounded another bend, and in the distance Barry suddenly saw a halo of brightness in the night sky. It must be the lights of Dublin. *Homeward bound*, he thought happily, glad that he would be able to reassure his mother – and, of course, Grace's mother – both of whom must be really worried at this stage. There would also be a bit of explaining to do to the police about the illegal entry to Pawlek's house, but he reckoned that that would fade into insignificance when they delivered their prize – a living, breathing Nazi spy!

He thought back to the night when the bombs had rained down on Liverpool and how he had sworn somehow to fight back. Was that really only a little over two months ago? So much had happened: his meeting up with Grace, the bullying by Shay McGrath, Johnny Keogh intervening, becoming pals with Charlie Dawson, Mum coming over on holidays. But most important of all was the fact that he *had* fought back, by acting on his suspicions that Pawlek was a spy.

He smiled in the darkened cab of the van, already figuring out how he would tell the story to Dad, then he drove on down the hillside and towards the beckoning lights of Dublin.

CHAPTER TWENTY-TWO

Grace wished that the summer didn't have to end. But it was the last week in August now and change was in the air. Next week she would be starting secondary school, and just a few days ago she had moved with Ma into their new house, a cottage on Olaf Road. Ma had decided not to return to the North Strand, and instead had chosen to rent a house in the Stoneybatter area. It meant that Grace could stay in Stanhope Street convent, she would still be near to Granddad, and she could continue being friends with the local children she had grown to know these last few months.

She had been something of a heroine when the initial fuss with the police had died down and the full story of Mr Pawlek had got out. May Bennett had breathlessly proclaimed that it was like something you'd see in the films in the Broadway Cinema. Charlie Dawson had insisted that she should have got a medal, and Whacker Wallace had said that Grace had done really well – though he himself would have riddled Pawlek with bullets. Even the ultra-tough Johnny Keogh had sought Grace out, and had told her that she was dead sound.

Grace smiled at the memories as she lay comfortably in bed in her new home, drowsy and almost ready for sleep. She thought back over the most eventful summer of her life and the adventures she had had with Barry. He was going home to Liverpool tomorrow, and she was going to miss him. But the air raids on Liverpool had died down to a trickle now, and she could understand why his mother wanted him back again. She hoped that they would stay really good friends, and that he would regularly visit his granny in Dublin, and that maybe she could even go to see him in Liverpool.

But all that was in the future. Now the story of this memorable summer was coming to a close, and so she closed her heavy eyelids and drifted easily into a deep and comfortable sleep.

The ship's horn blared, its deep-sounding blast scattering into flight the dockside pigeons that wheeled over the river Liffey. Barry stood near the gangway leading to the ferry, excited to be going home to Liverpool, but sorry to be leaving behind those to whom he had grown close. Being a Tuesday, it was a normal work day, and Barry had been touched that after putting in a day's work, people like Grace's mother and her Uncle Freddie had made the effort to come down to the docks to see him off. Also present were Grandma Peg, Grace's grandfather, Mr Ryan, and, of course, Grace herself.

Freddie had been his usual silly self, making corny jokes, but now that the time had come for goodbyes Barry couldn't help but feel a certain affection for him. Grace's mother had baked fruit scones for Barry to bring with him on the journey, Mr Ryan had given him a present of a jazz record for Mum, and Freddie had slipped him a half crown, insisting that he get himself a treat on the voyage home. Grandma Peg had been the most emotional, tearfully telling him how much she had loved having him stay with her.

'All aboard now! All aboard, please!' cried a uniformed ferry company officer.

Grandma Peg gave Barry a final hug, then there was a flurry of handshakes from Mr Ryan and Freddie, and hugs from Grace and her mother.

'Well…' said Barry, feeling a little emotional himself now that it was time to go.

'Mind yourself, Barry,' said Grace. 'And thanks for being such a brilliant friend!'

'You too, Grace,' he said his voice cracking slightly. 'You too.'

'All aboard, ladies and gentlemen, please!' said the uniformed officer.

Barry picked up his cardboard suitcase, gave a wave to the others and started up the gangplank. The ship was bustling with passengers and crew, and it took Barry a while to find a free spot on the ship's rail, from where he could look back down the quay-side towards his friends.

The ship's gangplank had already been pulled up, and now Barry heard the sound of the anchor being raised. The deep throb of the engines grew louder, then the ropes securing the vessel to the quayside capstans were undone and thrown on board. Slowly at first, then with increasing speed, the ship eased away from the quay and out into the river.

Barry could see Grandma Peg being comforted by Mr Ryan, while Freddie, Grace and Grace's mother all waved farewell. Barry waved in return as long as he could see them, then the ship changed tack a little, and they were lost to sight.

He stayed at the ship's rail as the vessel sailed down the Liffey. He felt a funny mixture of emotions – excitement to be allowed to travel alone, anticipation of the joy of arriving home again, and sadness at missing those he had left behind.

He looked back up the river at the city, bathed in early evening sunshine, and he knew that he would always savour the months he had spent there. He stood gazing back for a long time, lost in his thoughts, then he knew that this episode – the biggest adventure of his life so far – was over.

He turned away and looked downriver towards the open sea. The ship was picking up speed, and Barry allowed the warm, salty breeze to play over his face as he left behind the city of Dublin, and a summer he would never forget.

EPILOGUE

The Second World War went on for four more years before the Nazis were defeated in 1945 by the Allies. During the rest of the war Ireland's neutrality wasn't seriously breached by either side.

Mr Pawlek, who was identified as Wilhelm Schmidt, was tried and imprisoned in the Curragh Camp with other Germans captured in Ireland. In 1943, after two years in captivity, he escaped and made his way back to Germany. He served on the Eastern Front, but during the final days of the war, as the Red Army advanced on Berlin, he went missing and was never seen again.

Granddad lived into his nineties and played cards for many more years with Miss Kinsella.

Grandma Peg missed Barry badly, but found consolation in her religious faith. She lived to be seventy-nine, and was buried as she wished, in the robes of the Third Order.

Uncle Freddie never married, though some people jokingly said that Granddad and Freddie were like an old married couple, frequently arguing, yet happy in each other's company.

Ma and Grace settled contentedly in their new home. Three years later Ma got married again – with Grace's full approval – to the widower next door.

Charlie Dawson surprised no-one by growing up to be an

entertainer, and he had a long and successful career as a singer and comedian.

Shay McGrath and his family settled permanently in Birmingham. Drafted into National Service in the British Army, he was killed at the age of twenty-one in a skirmish with Malayan insurgents.

Johnny Keogh left school at fourteen and emigrated to America, where he worked as a security guard. In time he became head of security for a chain of restaurants. He particularly enjoyed the perk of free meals, and always relished his favourite dessert, rhubarb tart.

Barry's father was wounded in action with the Royal Navy. After recovering from his injures he was posted to a desk job with the navy's Western Command in Liverpool, where he was reunited with his family. After the war he was re-employed at the insurance company where he used to work, and he went on to be a general manager.

Uncle George survived the prison camp and came home after the war looking a little older and a lot thinner, but without having lost the sense of humour that Barry loved. He continued working as a van driver until his retirement.

Barry's mother worked on as a riveter, and was promoted to the role of supervisor by the end of the war. When the war ended she continued her new-found interest in engineering by attending night classes, and in time she qualified as a metalwork teacher, a role she enjoyed for many years.

Grace went on working part-time in Miss Kinsella's cake shop.

She took over running it, very successfully, when the older woman retired, and to her surprise and delight inherited the business when Miss Kinsella died.

Despite living permanently in Liverpool from 1941 onwards, Barry stayed friends with Grace and Charlie for the rest of his life. He became a senior detective in the police force, and over the course of his career solved many important cases. Privately, however, he admitted that no case was more memorable than his first one. A case he solved during a special summer in Dublin when he was twelve years old, and when he and Grace took on a Nazi spy – and won.

HISTORICAL NOTE

Secrets and Shadows is a work of fiction, but the historical elements are real, from the minor dramas of rationing – twelve ounces of butter a week for each person – to major events such as the blitz on Liverpool, the sinking of the Bismarck, and the bombing of the North Strand, all of which took place as described. However, the Ryan and Malone families are creations of my imagination, as is Mr Pawlek.

A number of German spies operated in Ireland during the Second World War but, unlike Mr Pawlek, most of them were soon rounded up. Ireland remained neutral for the duration of the war, in which it is estimated that over sixty million people died.

The North Strand area was rebuilt after the air raid and looks very different today. A monument and garden in the grounds of Marino College of Further Education commemorate those who were killed in the raid. Liverpool suffered badly from bombing during the war, and over 100,000 houses there were damaged.

The places where the events of the book happen, such as Arbour Hill, where Grace and Barry lived, Manor Street, where Mr Pawlek rented the house, and Stoneybatter, where Grace worked in the fictitious Kinsella's cake shop, are all actual places that still exist in Dublin.

Grace's new school, Stanhope Convent, and Barry's school, St

Paul's CBS in Brunswick Street, known as 'Brunner', both still function.

The Dublin Cattle Market at the North Circular Road closed in the 1970s, so children in Stoneybatter today can no longer share Grace's pleasure in seeing runaway cattle mounting the pavements.

Other locations in the story such as the garrison church, the sand dunes at Dollymount Strand and the Phoenix Park are actual places in Dublin and haven't changed a great deal since 1941.

Brian Gallagher,
Dublin 2012.

Other books by Brian Gallagher

Liam and Nora form an unlikely friendship when he helps her out during a music competition. Liam's father, a mechanic, is a proud trade union member, while Nora's father is a prosperous wine importer. When Jim Larkin takes on the might of the employers in 1913, resulting in strikes, riots and lockouts, Liam and Nora's loyalties are torn and their friendship challenged.

Annie Reilly wins a scholarship to Eccles Street School. There she makes friends with Susie O'Neill, and, through her, Peter Scanlon, a boy from a wealthy family who goes to school at Belvedere. But civil war is brewing in Ireland and hotheaded Peter has become involved in running messages for the rebels. When Annie is kidnapped, Peter is forced to make a terrible choice. Should he risk his life and betray his cause for Annie? And can they ever be friends again after this?

Twins Dylan and Emma Goldman move from Washington to Belfast when their journalist father is sent to cover the turbulent early days of the civil rights movement. The complicated friendships prove life-threatening when the simmering tensions in Northern Ireland erupt into violence in the summer of 1969.